THE ORDER OF THE UNICORN

THE IMAGINARY VETERINARY: BOOK 4

Emily

BY SUZANNE SELFORS
ILLUSTRATIONS BY DAN SANTAT

Little, Brown and Company

New York Boston

ALSO BY SUZANNE SELFORS:

The Imaginary Veterinary Series
The Sasquatch Escape
The Lonely Lake Monster
The Rain Dragon Rescue
The Order of the Unicorn
The Griffin's Riddle

To Catch a Mermaid
Fortune's Magic Farm

The Smells Like Dog Series
Smells Like Dog
Smells Like Treasure
Smells Like Pirates

Ever After High
Next Top Villain
General Villainy: A Destiny
Do-Over Diary

Text copyright © 2014 by Suzanne Selfors
Illustrations copyright © 2014 by Dan Santat
Text in excerpt from *The Griffin's Riddle* copyright © 2015 by Suzanne Selfors
Illustrations in excerpt from *The Griffin's Riddle* copyright © 2015 by Dan Santat

Little, Brown and Company

Hachette Book Group
1290 Avenue of the Americas, New York, NY 10104
Visit us at lb-kids.com

Little, Brown and Company is a division of Hachette Book Group, Inc.
The Little, Brown name and logo are trademarks of Hachette Book Group, Inc.

The publisher is not responsible for websites (or their content) that are not owned by the publisher.

First Paperback Edition: February 2015
First published in hardcover in July 2014 by Little, Brown and Company

Library of Congress Cataloging-in-Publication Data

Selfors, Suzanne.
    The Order of the Unicorn / by Suzanne Selfors ; illustrations by Dan Santat.—First edition.
       pages cm.—(The imaginary veterinary; book 4)
    Summary: "Ten-year-olds Pearl and Ben continue their apprenticeships at Dr. Woo's Worm Hospital as they travel with Dr. Woo to the Tangled Forest and the Dark Forest in search of a missing unicorn, and learn more about the villainous Maximus Steele"—Provided by publisher.
    ISBN 978-0-316-36406-5 (hc)—ISBN 978-0-316-32339-0 (library edition ebook)—ISBN 978-0-316-36410-2 (ebook)—ISBN 978-0-316-36407-2 (pb) [1. Unicorns—Fiction. 2. Imaginary creatures—Fiction. 3. Veterinarians—Fiction. 4. Apprentices—Fiction.] I. Santat, Dan, illustrator. II. Title.
    PZ7.S456922Or 2014
    [Fic]—dc23

                                                                        2013039049

10 9 8 7 6 5 4 3

RRD-C

Printed in the United States of America

For unicorns everywhere

CONTENTS

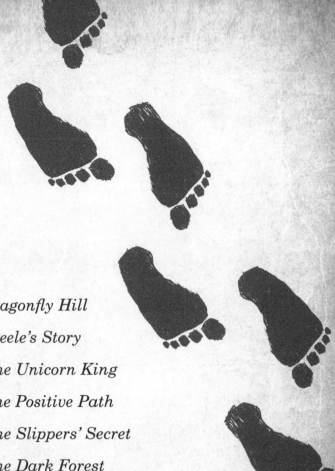

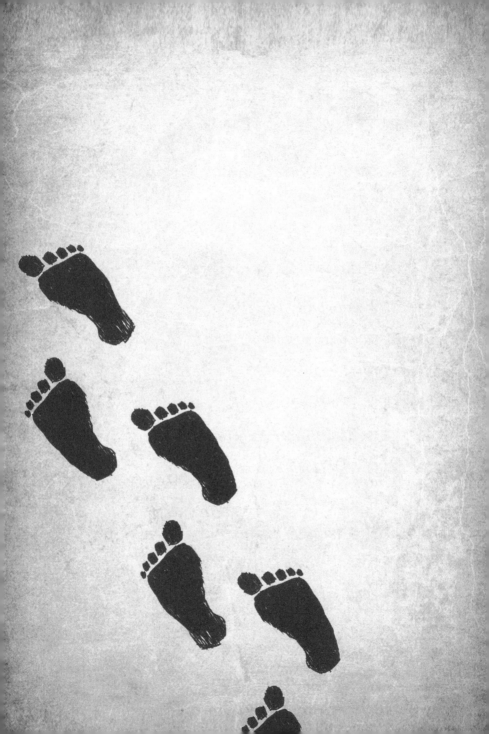

1

The first thing many people do after getting out of bed is put on a pair of slippers.

The first thing Pearl Petal did on that Friday morning was slip her feet into a pair of leprechaun shoes.

Shoes made by a real, living, breathing leprechaun.

They fit perfectly around her medium-sized feet. Pink was not her favorite color, but she wasn't about to complain. She'd been told by the leprechaun that the shoes did something special. But he hadn't told her *what*. This lack of information was keeping Pearl awake at night, and she found herself doing very strange things in an attempt to solve the mystery.

The shoes didn't make her fly—that's for sure. She'd tried wearing them while jumping off the kitchen counter and flapping her arms. She'd ended up with a twisted ankle and a scolding from her father. They didn't make her invisible. She'd tried sneaking into the kitchen for a late-night helping of ice cream. Her mother had looked right at her and said, "It's too late for sugar, young lady." They certainly didn't make Pearl strong. She'd tried lifting the car, but all she'd gotten were some weird looks from passersby.

Maybe Cobblestone the leprechaun was a big, fat liar. Or, in this case, a *little*, fat liar. Maybe the shoes did nothing at all.

Even if that proved to be true, no one else in Buttonville had shoes created by a cobbler from the Imaginary World. That fact in itself made Pearl smile.

After opening her bedroom window, Pearl stuck her head outside to see what the morning might bring. Across the street, a flock of pigeons preened their feathers as they perched on the Town Hall roof. The scent of sizzling bacon drifted up from the Buttonville Diner, and Mr. Wanamaker's keys jingled as he opened his barbershop. The morning sky was cloudless, which made Pearl happy. It was also dragonless, which made Pearl extra happy. No clouds meant sunshine. No dragons meant that certain secrets were still...*secret*.

She closed the window. Then her gaze swept across her bedroom shelves, which she'd filled with some of her prized possessions. Her bird-nest collection included nests from a blue jay, a robin, and a

hummingbird. But the pigeon's was the most beautiful because pigeons liked to decorate with ribbons, bits of plastic, and buttons.

Pearl's board game collection included Monopoly, Scrabble, and Pony Parade. The goal in Pony Parade was to move a plastic pony from the forest, where it was lost, to its home in the barn. Standing in the way were obstacles, such as a slippery banana peel, a pollywog pond, and a swarm of bees. If you landed on the golden square, you got to trade in your pony for a plastic unicorn. That was Pearl's favorite part. Although she'd outgrown the game, she still longed for a pony. She'd spent a great deal of time trying to persuade her parents to buy one. She imagined braiding its mane and riding it around town. When her parents pointed out that they didn't own a barn, Pearl said, "We can keep it in the alley." Mr. and Mrs. Petal hadn't liked that idea.

Pearl knelt on the carpet and opened the Pony Parade box. She'd hidden three very special pieces of paper inside: a certificate of merit in Sasquatch

Catching, a certificate of merit in Curing Lake Monster Loneliness, and a certificate of merit in Rescuing a Rain Dragon. Each certificate was signed by Dr. Emerald Woo, a veterinarian for Imaginary creatures. Now that she'd been working as Dr. Woo's apprentice, something as ordinary as a pony sounded boring. There were so many Imaginary creatures that could be kept in the alley!

"Pearl, Ben's here," her mom, Susan Petal, called from the kitchen.

"Okay. Coming!" As fast as she could, Pearl stuffed the certificates back in the box, then set the game on the shelf. She scrambled out of her pajamas and into her favorite clothes—a plain, well-worn T-shirt and a pair of shiny red basketball shorts. Then she pulled her blond hair into a ponytail and hurried to the kitchen.

"Hi, Ben."

"Hi, Pearl."

Ben Silverstein was sitting at the table. Pearl

had only known him for a week, but he'd become her very best friend in the whole world. After all, when two people travel together through interdimensional space, climb the face of a rain dragon, and seal up a hole in her head—not to mention stalk a sasquatch, save a dragon hatchling, and ride in a lake monster's mouth—they can't help but become best friends.

"So nice that you stopped by," Mrs. Petal told Ben. She was standing at the kitchen sink, rinsing the coffeepot. "How's your grandfather?"

"He's fine," Ben said, setting a napkin on his lap. "He's doing some stuff at the senior center this morning."

"Your grandfather's a very nice man." Mrs. Petal was already wearing her work apron, with its embroidered slogan: **YOU GET MORE AT THE DOLLAR STORE**. She dried her hands on a dish towel. "You kids eat as many pancakes as you like. I'll be unpacking a shipment from China." Then she walked down the stairs and disappeared into the Dollar Store, which the Petal family owned and operated.

Pearl sat down and grabbed two pancakes. She covered one with syrup, laid four strips of bacon across it, then set another pancake on top. Ben watched with wonder as she picked up her creation with both hands. "What?" she asked. "You've never made a pancake sandwich? It's delicious."

He looked around, as if making sure no one would scold him for bad manners. Then, with a shrug, Ben set aside his fork and grabbed two pancakes. His sandwich had jam in the middle.

"So, what kind of creatures do you think we'll meet today?" Pearl asked. This had become one of her favorite questions.

"Naw deeah," Ben said, which was really "no idea," but his mouth was stuffed.

"I hope we meet a fairy. I really, *really*, REALLY want to meet one." Pearl dipped her sandwich in more syrup. "What size do you think they are? Are they small like a housefly, or maybe big like a bat? Do you think they're pretty? Do you think they can speak our language? Do you—"

Her stream of questions came to a stop. She'd spied something on the table.

Something that made her blood boil.

2

CLUBS AND CROWNS

Pearl's blood didn't actually boil. That's just a way of saying that she felt so angry she got hot all over.

The morning newspaper lay neatly folded on the corner of the table. Staring right at her, from the front page, was Pearl's archenemy, Victoria Mulberry.

The photo showed Victoria's smiling face, her braces looking like railroad tracks. Thick glasses were perched on the end of her nose, and her frizzy hair was pressed beneath a baseball cap embroidered with the words WELCOME WAGON.

It wasn't unusual for Victoria to get her photo in the paper. She was always *achieving* one thing or another. She'd organized a search party when Mr. Mutt's dog went missing. She'd picked up garbage in the park after the storm of the century. She'd even raised money to help the seniors buy pudding for pudding day. Those were nice things to do, but Pearl knew the truth. The real person behind those deeds was Victoria's mother, Mrs. Mulberry, who'd made it her life's work to get her daughter's photo in the paper.

Pearl dropped her pancake sandwich and reached across the table. With sticky fingers, she unfolded the newspaper and read the following article aloud.

LOCAL GIRL WINS AWARD

The International Welcome Wagon Society has announced that Victoria Mulberry, age 10, is to become the newest member of the Red Wagon Club.

"This is a very important club," Victoria's mother, Martha Mulberry, said. "Only a few people are chosen each year. Victoria is a role model for kids everywhere."

When asked why she was a role model, Victoria replied, "I don't know," and went back to reading her book.

"Victoria earned this honor because she gets straight A's and she doesn't get into trouble like a certain other girl in our town," Mrs. Mulberry added.

The ceremony will be held at 6:00 PM Friday at Town Hall. A representative from the International Welcome Wagon Society will award Victoria with a special crown that is worn only by Red Wagon Club members. The entire town is invited to watch the ceremony. Cookies and punch will be served.

Pearl stared at the page. "'She doesn't get into trouble like a *certain other girl*,'" she repeated. "That's so rude."

"She probably wasn't talking about you," Ben said. He drank some orange juice.

"Of course she was talking about me." Pearl had a reputation. She was the town troublemaker, and everyone knew it, even Ben. "Why are they giving her a crown? That's crazy. Who wears a crown?"

"I don't know. A princess?"

"Yeah, well, Victoria's no princess." Pearl pushed the newspaper aside, then sat back in her chair. A bad feeling washed over her, as if a gray rain cloud had settled on top of her head. "Victoria's probably going to wear her crown all over town."

"So what if she does?" Ben asked.

Pearl frowned. Ben clearly didn't understand what it was like to grow up in a small town, with only a few kids in your grade. When you were labeled the local *troublemaker*, you couldn't get rid of that title, no matter how hard you tried. Just once it would be nice to see her own name on the front page and not followed by the words *mayhem*, *disaster*, or *trouble*.

"Pearl," Mrs. Petal called from downstairs. "Please take a pancake to your aunt Gladys before you leave."

"Okay," Pearl said. Then she glanced at the stove clock. "We'd better hurry or we'll be late."

While Pearl and her parents lived above the Dollar Store, her great-aunt Gladys lived in the apartment beneath. It wasn't a typical damp, cold basement with spiders, cobwebs, and mice. Gladys's place was warm, with a soft carpet, floral wallpaper, and two well-fed wiener dogs. The only thing odd was the smell.

"What is that?" Ben asked, scrunching his nose.

"Mentholated ointment," Pearl explained. "She rubs it all over because she has arthritis."

Aunt Gladys sat in a comfy chair, working a pair of knitting needles. The joints in her fingers were swollen and knotted. A ball of yellow yarn lay on her lap. Another waited at her feet. In fact, balls of yarn were scattered everywhere, as if a yarn factory had exploded in her living room. A soft *click-clack* arose from her wooden needles.

"Hi, Aunt Gladys. I brought your breakfast," Pearl announced. She pushed some yarn aside and set the plate on a TV tray.

"Thank you." Aunt Gladys looked up from her project, which appeared to be a hat. "Who is this nice young man?"

"This is my friend Ben," Pearl said.

"Hello," Ben said. Then he looked around. "Wow." Gladys had knitted practically everything in the apartment—the sofa cover, the wall hangings, the pillows, her clothes, and her slippers. She'd even covered her eyeglasses in yarn. The two rotund wiener dogs, who were snoozing on the couch, wore matching knitted sweaters. "You sure like to knit," Ben said, giving each dog a little pat on the head.

"I am the Queen of Knitting," Gladys told him. Then she reached under her chair and pulled out a small silver crown. She plopped it on top of her white curls. QUEEN OF THE KNITTING GUILD was engraved across the front. "Isn't it pretty?"

"Yes," Pearl said. "It's very pretty." As she wondered what Victoria's crown would look like, she got that rain cloud feeling again.

Aunt Gladys slid her project off the needles, tied a knot, and snipped the yarn with a pair of scissors.

Then she handed it to Ben. "A gentleman should always have a nice hat."

"Thank you," Ben said. He politely pulled the hat onto his head. Pearl wanted to giggle. The hat did not match Ben's fancy clothes. When she first met him, his sneakers had been brand-new, his pants perfectly pressed, and his shirt spotless. He was looking a bit wrinkly after a few days with his grandfather, but his clothes were still nicer than the stuff she got from the Dollar Store.

"We gotta go," Pearl said. She kissed her great-aunt's forehead. "Remember to eat your pancake."

"Bye-bye," Aunt Gladys said with a little wave. The wiener dogs raised their heads, shifted position, and went right back to sleep.

Pearl led the way up the stairs and through the store, where her parents were unpacking boxes.

"Did you see the article about Victoria?" Mr. Petal asked. His box was full of pencils.

"The ceremony is tonight," Mrs. Petal said. Her box contained sunglasses. "I think we should all go."

"Do we have to?" Pearl asked with a groan.

"Yes, we do," Mrs. Petal said. "It's nice to support our fellow Buttonvillers. If you'd done something special, you'd want people to support you."

But I have done something special, Pearl thought. She glanced at Ben. They'd both done tons of special things, thanks to Dr. Woo. Unfortunately, no one could ever know.

"Thanks for breakfast," Ben said just before he and Pearl headed out the door.

"Have fun at the worm hospital," Mr. Petal called.

Pearl smiled, revealing the big gap between her teeth. So what if Victoria got to be in the Red Wagon Club? Nobody but Ben and Pearl got to work as apprentices in a secret hospital for Imaginary creatures.

But deep inside, Pearl still thought it would be nice if the people in town thought she was more than just a troublemaker.

3

MAIL-ORDER WORMS

It might have been a short walk to Dr. Woo's hospital had it not been for a bright red obstruction.

"Stop right there." The bossy voice belonged to Mrs. Mulberry, who stood directly in their path. She wore red overalls and a matching red baseball cap with the words WELCOME WAGON printed on it. This was her uniform, for she was the president of Buttonville's Welcome Wagon Committee, a group dedicated to welcoming newcomers. But ever since the old button factory closed down, people rarely moved to Buttonville. So Mrs. Mulberry found other things to do—like spying on everyone who already lived there. She was a professional busybody. "I suppose you two are on your way to Dr. Woo's Worm Hospital," she said.

"We can't talk right now," Pearl said. What she really meant was, *We don't want to talk to you*, but that would be a rude thing to say. "We're in a hurry."

"We don't want to be late," Ben added.

Mrs. Mulberry was an expert at blocking people's paths. She stood, legs wide apart, in the center of the sidewalk, holding out her arms like a traffic cop. A small red wagon was parked next to her. "Not so fast. I've got a few questions for you two."

Drat! Pearl groaned. "Fine, but please make it quick."

Ben stood at Pearl's side. They'd dealt with Mrs. Mulberry before. Ever since Dr. Woo moved into the old button factory, Mrs. Mulberry had been trying to make an appointment to meet her. She was curious about Dr. Woo and desperate to snoop inside the hospital. So far, she hadn't been successful, and the apprentices were determined to keep it that way.

Mrs. Mulberry narrowed her eyes. "How is the doctor?"

"Fine," Pearl said.

"If she's fine, how come nobody in town has ever seen her?"

"My grandfather met her," Ben pointed out. "So did Pearl's mom."

"Well, I haven't." Mrs. Mulberry folded her arms and scowled. "I'm mighty suspicious about this hospital of hers. I asked around. No one in Buttonville has a pet worm. So why would Dr. Woo come all the way from Iceland to open a worm hospital in a place where no one keeps worms?"

Pearl didn't have a good answer. She looked at Ben. He was quite talented at making up stories on the spot. He cleared his throat, buying time. Then,

with a smile, he said, "Iceland is full of volcanoes, and Dr. Woo got tired of shoveling lava off her front porch. That's why she moved."

Mrs. Mulberry scowled so hard a deep crease formed across her forehead. "But why would she only treat worms? Why not dogs and cats?"

"She..." Ben closed his eyes for a moment, as if conjuring the details for his story. "She only takes care of worms because..." His eyes popped open. "Because when she was young, her father was a fisherman, and you know what fishermen do to worms, don't you? They stab a hook right through them, then dangle them into the water. Dr. Woo thought this was unfair, so she decided to dedicate her life to undoing all the wrongs done to worms."

"Wow," Pearl said, snickering. "That's a great story." Then she looked at Mrs. Mulberry and added in a serious tone, "And *totally* true."

Mrs. Mulberry reached into her wagon and picked up a catalog for gardening supplies. "Well, Dr. Woo won't see me unless I have a worm, so I've ordered an entire box of red compost worms. It's coming special order."

"Uh..." Pearl started to fidget. On the one hand, she was worried about being late to the apprenticeship. On the other hand, Mrs. Mulberry had to be stopped! If she got into the hospital and saw the creatures that were hidden inside, the secret would be out and Dr. Woo would have to leave Buttonville. How could Pearl stop this from happening? "Uh..."

"Dr. Woo only sees sick worms," Ben said.

"Right," Pearl agreed. *Good point. Problem solved.* "Well, we gotta go."

"Hold on. There's bound to be one sick worm in the box." Mrs. Mulberry glanced around, then asked, "How can I tell if a worm is sick?"

"Coughing," Ben said.

"Sneezing, too," Pearl added, clenching her jaw so she wouldn't laugh.

"Coughing? Sneezing? I knew that." Mrs. Mulberry dropped the catalog back into the wagon. "I expect to see both of you at Victoria's ceremony tonight.

Membership in the Red Wagon Club is highly selective. This is an important moment for the Mulberry family. Don't be late."

"Late?" Pearl cried. She grabbed Ben's wrist and stared at his fancy watch. "We gotta go!"

4

B en and Pearl skidded to a stop outside the tall
wrought-iron gate that guarded the old button
factory. A heavy padlock hung from the bars,
along with a sign that read:

WELCOME TO DR. WOO'S WORM HOSPITAL.
DR. WOO DOES NOT TREAT CATS, DOGS, PIGS, RATS,
SNAKES, TURTLES, FISH, FROGS, OR ANY
OTHER CREATURE THAT IS NOT A WORM.
DR. WOO SEES WORMS BY APPOINTMENT ONLY.
IF YOU DON'T HAVE AN APPOINTMENT,
→ **KEEP OUT!** ←

Fortunately, Pearl and Ben had an appointment. Their apprenticeships were scheduled to begin at precisely 8:00 AM.

"We're two minutes early," Ben reported.

"Early is better than late," Pearl said. She didn't want to give Dr. Woo a reason to fire her. With her hands wrapped around the bars, Pearl peered through the gate, watching for the hospital's front door to open. Would Mr. Tabby come get them, or would Dr. Woo?

The concrete building, which had once housed the Buttonville Button Factory, stood ten stories high. Many of the windows were broken. The grounds surrounding the structure had been neglected, so weeds grew up to Pearl's knees. In its glory days, the button factory had been filled with the sounds of machinery grinding, people chatting, and delivery trucks coming and going. Now only an occasional growl escaped through the broken panes. The place looked like a hotel for ghosts.

At eight o'clock precisely, the doorknob turned. Pearl's heart did a little flutter. This was always an exciting moment, anticipation building like steam in a kettle. The front door opened and out stepped Dr. Woo's assistant, Mr. Tabby. He always looked like a butler, and today was no different. He wore a pair of perfectly pressed black pants, a crisp white shirt, and a burgundy velveteen vest. His long red hair was tied back in a ribbon, and his mustache was waxed into individual strands. As he strode down the driveway, gravel crunched beneath his polished black shoes.

"What's he carrying?" Pearl asked.

"Looks like a suitcase," Ben said.

Indeed, while one of Mr. Tabby's hands held a ring of keys, the other pulled a wheeled plaid bag. Pearl and Ben stepped back while Mr. Tabby unlocked the padlock. The brass key ring reminded Pearl of the kind that bulls wore in their snouts. Then Mr. Tabby swung open the gate. "Good morning," he said, his nose sniffing the air. A low growl vibrated in his throat. "Do I detect the scent of dachshund?"

"Dach-*what*?" Pearl asked.

"That's the official name for wiener dogs," Ben

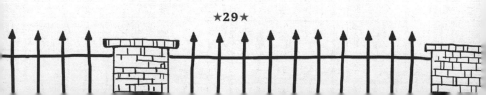

explained. Then he held his palms up to Mr. Tabby's nose. "I petted a pair of them."

"They belong to my great-aunt Gladys," Pearl told him. "Wow, you've sure got a good sniffer."

"I am not fond of dogs, wiener or otherwise." Mr. Tabby's upper lip curled with disgust. "Canines are drooling creatures that do their business on public sidewalks. Very distasteful." He leaned close to Ben. "What sort of hat is that?"

"Oh, I forgot I was wearing it," Ben said, pulling the knitted yellow cap from his head.

"My great-aunt Gladys made it," Pearl said. "She's made me one in every color. Do you want her to make you one?"

Mr. Tabby stroked one of his mustache sections. "I am not fond of hats, knitted or otherwise. They tend to mess up my hair." He rolled his suitcase onto the sidewalk.

"Are you leaving?" Ben asked, stuffing the hat into his back pocket.

"Indeed. I am taking my once-a-year vacation."

"Where are you going?" Pearl asked. She and her

family rarely took vacations. They worked so hard at the Dollar Store that it was difficult to get away.

"I am visiting a luxurious spa, where I will get a manicure, a pedicure, and a relaxing scalp massage." Was he making a purring sound? "It is very stressful being the assistant to the world's only veterinarian for Imaginary creatures. Too much stress can make my fur fall out."

"Fur?" Pearl asked. "Did you say...*fur*?"

Mr. Tabby glanced away. "I never said such a thing."

A taxicab pulled up to the curb. The driver got out. "You the gentleman I'm supposed to take to the airport?"

"That is correct, my good man." Mr. Tabby smiled politely. He handed his suitcase to the driver, who put it into the taxi's trunk. While the driver climbed back into the cab, Mr. Tabby gave the key ring to Ben. "Be certain to lock the gate, and do not forget to—"

"I know, I know," Ben interrupted. "Don't forget to lock the front door. You don't have to keep

★32★

reminding me." Ben was a bit sensitive about this subject. He'd neglected to lock the front door the first time he and Pearl visited the hospital, resulting in the escape of a sasquatch.

Mr. Tabby's mustache twitched. "It is my duty to remind you of such things, especially in light of the new situation." His yellow irises flashed.

A little shiver tickled the back of Pearl's neck. "What *situation*?"

"My trip is ill-timed, I'm afraid, but Dr. Woo insists I go." Mr. Tabby looked over his shoulder. The taxi driver sat inside the car, paying no attention to the conversation. Mr. Tabby motioned for the kids to gather close. As they looked up at him, he lowered his voice in a secretive way. "There has been a sighting."

"A what?" Ben asked.

"A sighting. In the Imaginary World. Of a *human*."

Pearl and Ben looked at each other. Mr. Tabby had said the word *human* as if he were talking about a piece of food that had gone rancid.

Mr. Tabby continued. "Because we do not know

★33★

how the human entered the Imaginary World, we must increase our security efforts. The hospital gate and front door are to remain locked at all times."

Ben's cheeks went red. "I won't leave it unlocked again. I promise."

"And rules are to be followed *at all times*. Do you understand?"

Pearl didn't argue. She and Ben had been apprentices for less than a week, and already they'd broken more rules than she could remember, including traveling through the Portal without permission and taking the leprechaun out of the hospital.

"Yes," they both replied. "We understand."

"Very good. Now, do you remember your task for today?" He tapped his shoe against the sidewalk as he waited for their reply.

"Yes," Ben said. "We have to trim the sasquatch's nose hairs."

"To precisely one-fourth inch in length," Mr. Tabby added.

Pearl groaned. "Ugh. That sounds super disgusting. Do we have to?"

"Do you have to?" Mr. Tabby's mustache twitched again. "Need I remind you that on Wednesday you did not dispose of dragon droppings in the correct manner—hence, your punishment?"

"Okay," Pearl said. She really couldn't argue about this. After all, it had been her idea to toss the droppings over the edge of the roof.

"You will find the trimming device in the Supply Closet. It requires ten batteries. Sasquatch nasal foliage is very stubborn and thick." He turned briskly on his heels and strode toward the cab. After slipping inside, he rolled down the window and gave Ben and Pearl one last piece of information. "In light of the dangerous situation, I installed extra security behind the front door. Good day."

"Dangerous?" Ben asked. He and Pearl watched as the cab drove away. "How dangerous?"

One thing Pearl had learned about Ben Silverstein was that he didn't like danger. He didn't like breaking rules, either. "I'm sure he was exaggerating," Pearl said, trying to make Ben feel better. "Come on. Let's go in."

Ben locked the gate, checking it twice to make sure it was secure, and then they headed up the driveway. "Do you think the situation is dangerous because the *human* is dangerous?" The ring of keys dangled from Ben's fingertips. "Or do you think it's dangerous because someone else knows how to get into the Imaginary World?"

"I'm not sure," Pearl said with a shrug. "But I had nothing to do with it." She was so used to people pointing fingers, accusing her of making trouble, that defending herself was a natural reaction. "I would never tell anyone how to get into the Imaginary World."

"Me neither," Ben said.

Pearl believed him. She had no reason not to. Sure, Ben liked to make up stories, but it made no sense that he'd spill any of Dr. Woo's secrets. Neither one of them wanted to risk losing their apprenticeships.

They walked up the steps and stood facing the front door. A familiar sign was taped to the outside:

THE WORM HOSPITAL IS
CLOSED
UNTIL IT IS
OPEN.

But there was something new about the door—a small hole had been drilled into it.

"A peephole?" Ben said. "That's the extra security?"

Pearl was about to tell Ben to use the key, but that was when an eyeball appeared on the other side of the peephole.

A loud growl slithered out the crack at the bottom of the door.

5

GUARD DRAGON

The ominous growl sent a vibration up Pearl's legs. *What* was behind the door?

Had something nasty escaped from one of the treatment rooms? Or had Mr. Tabby placed a monster in the lobby to scare off possible intruders? Pearl's heart kicked up its rhythm. Ben's face went pale. He stepped back as the beast stared through the peephole. But Pearl wasn't so quick to retreat. There was something familiar about that eyeball.

The growling stopped and the eyeball disappeared. Then came the sound of a dead bolt sliding open.

"Maybe we should go," Ben whispered.

"We're supposed to be here," Pearl whispered back. "Mr. Tabby wouldn't send something to hurt us." Yet how could she be so sure? She'd only known Mr. Tabby for a week, and he was usually quite grumpy. Maybe they'd broken another rule and this was their punishment?

The second dead bolt released. Then the third, fourth, and fifth.

The door opened.

"Did I scare you with my big, mean growl?" a voice asked. "Did I, huh? Did I?"

The black dragon who lived on the hospital roof stood hunched in the doorway. Pearl and Ben exhaled at the same time. This was no monster.

"Metalmouth!" Pearl exclaimed. "You nearly scared the pants off Ben."

"No, he didn't," Ben said, wiping sweat from his forehead.

The dragon smiled and *thwapp*ed his tail. "I'm supposed to guard the front door while Mr. Tabby's gone." He stepped aside so Pearl and Ben could enter. Pearl still couldn't believe that she knew a dragon. And this one talked! He slammed the door shut. Then, using his claws, he slid all the dead bolts into place.

"Did you hear about the human who got into the Imaginary World?" he asked. "Did you?"

"Yeah. Who do you think it is?" Pearl asked.

"Beats me." Metalmouth sat on his haunches. His head nearly reached the ceiling. He wasn't the largest dragon the kids had met, but he was big enough to take up most of the lobby. "I don't like watching the front door. What if an angry peasant wants to get in?" He'd seen a picture of rake-wielding villagers in a book called *History of Dragons* by Dr. Emerald Woo. There was also a drawing of a knight in shining armor attacking a dragon with a sword. No wonder Metalmouth was scared. Pearl figured it was a good thing he was living in Buttonville, where no one owned a sword—at least, not as far as she knew.

Pearl didn't want to scare Metalmouth, of course, but he needed to know something very important. "There is one person who might try to get inside the hospital. Her name is Martha Mulberry. She's a busybody."

Ben nodded. "My grandfather says she kvetches too much."

"Kvetches?" Metalmouth scratched his left ear. "What's that?"

"She complains. She whines. Grandpa Abe says we need Mrs. Mulberry about as much as we need holes in our heads."

"Oh, I don't want a hole in my head." Metalmouth flattened his ears and glanced at the door. "Do you think we should get some more locks? Huh? Do you?"

Even though he was big enough to sit on anyone who might try to sneak in, Metalmouth was about as gentle as a butterfly.

"I'm sure everything will be okay," Pearl told him. But she wasn't sure. What if Mrs. Mulberry brought the police? Or what if the *human* who'd been spotted in the Imaginary World tried to get in? Ben, who'd

been frowning since Mr. Tabby had used the word *dangerous* earlier, didn't seem sure, either.

"We have a security system in our house in Los Angeles," Ben said. "It sounds an alarm if any windows or doors are opened. I think Dr. Woo should get something like that, don't you?"

"But what happens if *you* open a window or door?" Pearl asked.

"I'm supposed to type a password into the keypad to turn off the alarm. But sometimes I forget, and then the guards come." Ben shrugged. "I usually tell them a story. One time I said that we had a ghost who couldn't make up his mind if he wanted to haunt the house or the yard, so he kept going in and out."

Pearl thought that was a funny story and might have laughed if Metalmouth's ears weren't still flattened. "I don't think I can watch all the windows *and* all the doors. I wish Mr. Tabby would come back," Metalmouth said.

Pearl reached out and patted the dragon's paw. "It'll be okay. Just make that big, mean growl, and no one will come anywhere near the hospital."

"Like this?" The dragon opened his mouth, exposing a row of teeth sharp enough to bite through metal. Pearl and Ben plugged their ears as a roar filled the lobby. Hot breath blew across their faces. If the building weren't made of concrete, the walls might have collapsed.

"Yeah," Pearl said after the roar stopped echoing. "Just like that."

Ben checked his watch. "We'd better get to work." He held out the ring of keys. "I guess I should leave this with you." Metalmouth opened a front paw. Ben slipped the ring over one of the dragon's claws.

"Don't melt it," Pearl said. The dragon had a habit of stealing metal objects and melting them into works of art. "Mr. Tabby wouldn't like that."

"Okay." Metalmouth tucked the key ring beneath one of his scales. Steam wafted from his nostrils. Thanks to his hot breath, the lobby was heating up like a sauna. Pearl wiped sweat drops from the back of her neck. The dragon pulled a yellow tennis ball from behind another scale. "Wanna play fetch?" His tongue rolled out of his mouth, and his tail *thwapp*ed again. "Huh? Wanna?"

"We can't," Ben said. "We have to go up to the Forest Suite and trim the sasquatch's nose hair."

"Sorry," Pearl said, feeling bad that they didn't have time to hang out. She really liked Metalmouth.

He was like a gigantic puppy. She couldn't have a dog, because her dad was allergic. But playing fetch with a dragon was a million times better.

Metalmouth sighed, and more hot air filled the room. "Okay. See you guys later."

He pressed his paw against the EMPLOYEES ONLY door, which used some sort of fingerprint-recognition technology. It clicked open.

"Thanks," Ben and Pearl said. They stepped through, and the door closed behind them.

Ben and Pearl walked down a long hallway until they reached the time clock, where they punched in. The time cards kept track of the apprentices' comings and goings. Violet, the switchboard operator, had already punched in. She worked on the tenth floor, where she fielded calls from the Imaginary World. Her card was thumbtacked to the ON DUTY side of the bulletin board. Ben placed his card and Pearl's card next to Violet's. Mr. Tabby's card was tacked to the OFF DUTY side, as was Vinny's. Pearl and Ben hadn't yet met him. Or her. Or it, as the case might be.

The next step was to put on their white lab coats. They'd been soaked after the trip to the Land of Rain, but now they were nice and dry. "Hey, what's this?" Pearl asked. A note was taped to her lapel.

Apprentices,
come join me in
the basement.

—Dr. Woo

"I wonder what's going on in the basement," Pearl said.

Ben buttoned his coat. "Do you think we should take care of the sasquatch first?"

"No way." Pearl would do practically anything to get out of sticking her finger up a sasquatch's nose.

"But Mr. Tabby said—"

"Dr. Woo is the boss," Pearl interrupted. "Besides, aren't you dying to see what she keeps down there?"

She smiled. "Maybe it's something that likes to live underground, in the dark. Or something so big it won't fit in one of the regular rooms. Oooh, what could it be?"

Ben chewed on his lip. "I guess we're about to find out."

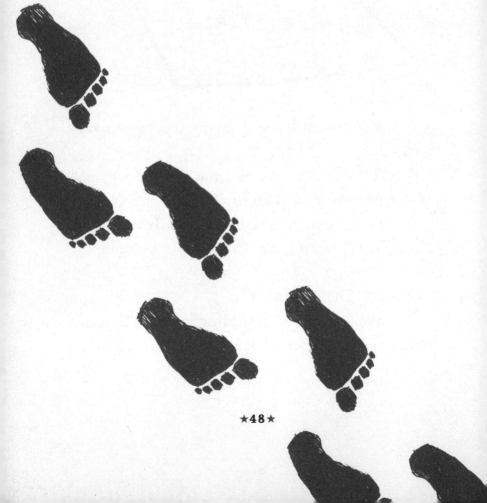

6

THE POOL BENEATH

Pearl and Ben hurried down the hallway to the stairwell. Pearl was so excited she felt like dancing. On Wednesday, they'd gone all the way to the roof, where Metalmouth lived. Then they'd visited the tenth floor, where they'd met Violet and encountered the amazing fairy-dust-powered Portal. But on this day, they'd be traveling in the opposite direction. What would they find?

The basement staircase was narrow and wound around and around like a corkscrew. No overhead

lights guided the way. "I can't see anything," Ben complained.

"Use the railing," Pearl told him. She'd taken the lead, which she tended to do. As she reached out carefully, right foot, then left foot, her eyes began to adjust. Water dripped down the stone walls. The dank air was heavy with the scent of rust. The corkscrew tightened. Just when Pearl began to feel dizzy, the staircase took its last turn. At the bottom, Pearl and Ben stepped onto a stone platform.

"Wow," Pearl said.

They were standing at the edge of a cavern the size of a football field. Torches burned along the perimeter, casting an orange glow on the water. The entire room was like a giant indoor swimming pool. Pearl instantly imagined filling her great-aunt Gladys's basement apartment with water. What fun that would be. The wiener dogs could float around on air mattresses, and Pearl could go swimming anytime she wanted. She might even raise koi fish, like the ones in Mr. Mutt's backyard pond. Those things were the size of cats.

Ben leaned over and dipped his fingers into the water. "It's pretty warm. I wish I'd brought my snorkel."

A floating dock led from the platform down the middle of the pool, and there, with a bucket by her side, sat Dr. Woo. "Over here," she called, her voice echoing off the stone walls.

Pearl smiled. She had a ton of questions to ask, and the sooner she could get started, the more likely she'd get answers. But when she stepped onto the dock, it lurched beneath her weight. "Whoa," she cried, almost falling over.

"You'll get used to it," Dr. Woo said. "Just take slow steps."

Pearl and Ben struggled to keep their balance as the floating dock shifted and swayed. Pearl wanted to look in the water to see what might be swimming around, but she didn't dare take her eyes off her feet. Luckily, her leprechaun shoes were thin enough that she was able to grip the dock with her toes.

"We got your note," Ben said when they finally reached the doctor.

"Please, sit down," she told them.

Like her apprentices, Dr. Emerald Woo wore a white laboratory coat. She'd rolled up her pants and was sitting with her legs dangling in the pool. Her long black hair cascaded over her shoulders. A deep scar ran across her cheek, another down her neck. How she'd gotten them was still a mystery. Pearl intended to ask that question, but right now there were other questions bouncing in her brain like Ping-Pong balls.

"What are we doing down here?" she asked. "What's in the water? Should I go home and get my swimsuit? We sell flippers at the Dollar Store. Should I go get those, too?"

"We just ate a big pancake breakfast," Ben added. "Aren't you supposed to wait an hour after eating so you don't get cramps?"

"I won't get cramps," Pearl said. She started to take off her leprechaun shoes.

"Keep your shoes on, Pearl. You and Ben won't be swimming today." Torchlight flickered in her black eyes. "As a matter of fact, it would be extremely

dangerous for either you or Ben to put any part of your body in the water."

"*Extremely* dangerous?" Ben asked, scooting away from the edge of the dock.

"Only if you enter the water. If you stay here on the dock, you are perfectly safe." She moved her feet in gentle circles.

"But you're in the water," Pearl pointed out. "I mean, you're *half* in the water. How come it's not extremely dangerous for you?"

"I will explain that shortly," Dr. Woo said. "This cavern is where I treat the most deadly of the water-dwelling creatures." Ben gulped so loud it sounded as if he'd swallowed a rock. "If we sit quietly, it will show itself."

Did they want it to show itself? This was another important question ricocheting in Pearl's mind, but she didn't let it escape. Overcome with curiosity, she sat absolutely still. The most deadly water-dwelling creature she could think of was a shark. Or an electric eel. What could this possibly be?

They sat in silence, waiting and watching for

something to change. Nothing could be seen below the surface of the dark green water, not even Dr. Woo's legs. Ben gripped his kneecaps, his eyes darting around. Pearl tried her best to be quiet, but after a few minutes, she felt as if she might explode from boredom.

Then a bubble appeared. And another. A string of bubbles formed, each one a little closer to the dock. "It's coming this way," Ben whispered.

Pearl didn't know what to expect. She wanted to squeal with excitement, but she clamped her jaw tight so she wouldn't make any noise. This was worse than waiting for someone to jump out and say "boo!" Ben clenched his hands as he stared at the bubbles.

A dark spot appeared. It was the top of something's head, and it slowly rose from the water.

Pearl gasped. She had no idea what she was looking at.

Correction—she had no idea what was looking at *her*.

7

KID SANDWICHES

Is that a horse?" Ben whispered.

"Of course it's not a horse," Pearl said. "Horses don't swim underwater." But then she realized that the two wet eyes looking right at her were horse eyes, on a horse face, at the end of a horse neck. "Wait a minute...."

"You are correct, Pearl. The creature before you is not a horse, though it is a distant relative." Dr. Woo brought her legs out of the water and knelt on the dock. "This is a kelpie."

While the kelpie had a face and a mane like a

regular horse, its color was greenish black, perfectly matching the water. Its skin looked smooth, like a seal's.

The creature swam closer. "It's so cute," Pearl said. She reached out, but Dr. Woo grabbed her hand in midair. "I was just going to pet it," Pearl explained.

"Never try to pet a kelpie," Dr. Woo said gently.

"How come?"

"Because kelpies eat children."

"What?" The dock rocked as Ben shot to his feet. "Are you kidding?" His voice cracked.

Eat children? Pearl took a longer look and realized that the creature's stare was cold and calculating—the way a tiger might watch a bunny just before the pounce. Was the kelpie imagining what Pearl would look like inside a hamburger bun? Or between two pancakes? Pearl scooted away from the edge.

"Kelpies live in lakes and rivers," Dr. Woo explained. "Their front legs end in fins, and their hindquarters are serpent-like. They have the ability to shape-shift in order to catch their prey."

"Shape-shift?" Ben asked.

"When a kelpie walks onto land in the Imaginary World, it makes itself look like an ordinary horse. Then it offers a ride to a passing child. Once the child climbs onto its back, it carries him into the depths of the lake and drowns him. And then it feasts."

"That's horrible," Pearl said, glaring at the kelpie. It glared right back. She wanted to scold it. There were lots of other things to eat—why pick on children? *Do we taste good?* she wondered.

"Wait a minute," Ben said. "How can there be children in the Imaginary World? I thought humans didn't live there."

"That is a good point," Dr. Woo said. "However, there are many beings that have children. Elves, for instance. And trolls." She tucked her hair behind her ears. "The only way to tell a real horse from a kelpie—on land—is that the kelpie's mane will never stop dripping water."

The kelpie moved past Pearl and focused on Ben. It cocked its head, watching him with a stare that could turn a dragon flame to ice. "Uh, what level is it on the danger scale?" Ben asked. He looked ready to run to the exit. "Mr. Tabby said we'd need more training before we could be around a level four." The danger scale was how Mr. Tabby measured the creatures—one being tame, five being the most dangerous. Pearl guessed that anything that eats kids would rank a level five.

"The kelpie is a five-plus," Dr. Woo said.

"A five-plus?" Ben's voice cracked again. Pearl's stomach tightened. She and Ben hadn't yet met anything that was a level five. She wondered if the kelpie could leap from the water like a fish and grab her with its teeth. She balled her hands into fists, ready to defend herself if needed. No one was going to make a breakfast sandwich out of her!

"Ben, please sit down. You're rocking the dock." Dr. Woo patted the planks. "The kelpie will not eat you—at least not today. It is here to get treatment for an infected fin, and it has promised to behave." She patted the dock again. Ben looked totally unconvinced, but he sat anyway, his back as stiff as wood. The kelpie flared its nostrils and sniffed. Then it bobbed its head.

"What's it doing?" Pearl asked.

"It likes the way Ben smells," Dr. Woo explained. The kelpie sniffed again, then paddled closer.

"You'd better stop smelling me," Ben told the creature. He pointed his finger. "Because I am *not* on the menu."

"Actually, you are," Dr. Woo said with a sly smile.

Ben's mouth fell open. Pearl gasped. "You're joking, right?" she asked. "You just said it wouldn't eat us today."

"In order to recover from its infection, the kelpie needs nourishment. The problem is, it has completely lost its appetite." Dr. Woo reached into the bucket and pulled out a small fish. "Because children are a rare treat, the kelpie mostly eats fish, but I haven't been able to coax it into having any. I thought that by bringing you here, your scent might stimulate its appetite."

Pearl had to think about this for a moment. "You mean like when I smell a ripe nectarine and my mouth starts to water?"

"Exactly," Dr. Woo said.

"You want me to make its mouth water?" Ben cringed. Dr. Woo nodded.

"That kinda makes sense," Pearl said. "But I

don't understand why you're helping something that's so dangerous."

"It is not my job to judge what deserves to live and what deserves to die," Dr. Woo said, her brow furrowed. "All creatures have the right to medical care."

Pearl felt bad for asking the question. But she wasn't sure she agreed with Dr. Woo's answer. Did a flea deserve to live after it had sucked her blood?

The kelpie gazed coldly at Ben. "It definitely prefers Ben's scent," Dr. Woo said. "So if you wouldn't mind?" She held out the fish.

"You want me to...to..." He looked desperately at the doctor. "You can't be serious?"

"Of course I'm serious. I don't have a bottle labeled SCENT OF CHILDREN, so this is the best solution I can think of. I'm lucky to have you here."

"Look," Pearl said. "Its mouth is already watering." A little string of drool hung from the kelpie's lip.

"But what if it bites more than the fish?" Ben asked.

"I don't think it will."

"You don't *think*?" Ben frowned. "Is this how you lost your finger?"

Dr. Woo glanced at her right hand, which was missing an index finger. "No, I did not lose my finger to a kelpie." Then she wiggled the fish. "Please, Ben, I need your help."

Ben took the little fish. "What do I do?"

"Hold it out."

His hand shaking, he stretched his arm out and offered the fish to the kelpie. Pearl put both of her hands over her face, watching from between her fingers. If Ben got eaten, his grandfather would be furious with Dr. Woo.

The kelpie sniffed again. Then it pulled back its upper lip and opened its mouth. Ben squeezed his eyes shut. Pearl expected the creature to chomp down on the fish, but ever so delicately, the kelpie sucked it between its teeth. Then it swallowed the fish whole. Ben opened his eyes and lowered his hand.

"It didn't even chew," Pearl said. "I get into trouble if I don't chew. My mom says that I'll swallow too

much air and get gassy." The kelpie burped. "See."

Ben fed the kelpie another fish, then another. His hand shook every time, but he kept his eyes open. "Let me try," Pearl said, but the kelpie turned its head away, ignoring Pearl as if she were a piece of burned toast. "Hey," Pearl said, "how come it doesn't like the way I smell?"

"Kelpies tend to be fonder of boys."

"Well, that's not fair," Pearl grumbled.

"You're upset because she wants to eat me and not you?" Ben asked. "That's crazy."

Maybe so, Pearl thought. But she didn't like being left out.

After eating a dozen fish, the kelpie disappeared beneath the water. Dr. Woo reached into her lab coat pocket and removed her creature calculator—a device both she and Mr. Tabby used to keep track of their patients. She typed on the keypad, then read the screen. "Its energy level has improved already. I think it's going to be fine. Good job, Ben."

With a proud smile, Ben carried the empty bucket

as Dr. Woo led the way back up the dock. By the time they reached the stairwell, Pearl had conjured a bunch of new questions. "Dr. Woo, why do kelpies want to eat kids? Do kids taste different from grown-ups? How come they are fonder of boys? Are kelpies related to sea horses? How long do they live? If a kelpie grabs you, how do you escape?"

Dr. Woo turned around and smiled patiently. "Pearl, your questions are important, but they are as plentiful as scales on a dragon's back. Have you ever heard the saying 'Quality, not quantity'?"

"No," Pearl said.

"I have," said Ben. "It means that it's better to ask one great question instead of a hundred ordinary questions."

"Exactly." The doctor folded her arms, waiting for Pearl to decide.

"Fine." Pearl screwed up her face. One question. "Why should I care about something that wants to eat me?"

Dr. Woo raised her eyebrows. "Now *that* is an

exceptional question, but one you must answer yourself."

Before Pearl could point out that because there'd been no answer, she should get the chance to ask a second question, a nasal voice shot out of a wall speaker.

"Dr. Woo to the tenth floor immediately."

8

THE BROKEN BLESSING

A call has come in from the Imaginary World," Dr. Woo said. "I must go."

Great news! Pearl thought. She darted in front of the doctor and blocked the stairs. "Can we come with you?" Torchlight flickered in the distance. The pool was calm, the kelpie still submerged. "Please?"

"Come with me?" Dr. Woo pursed her lips. "You still haven't been properly trained to travel to the Imaginary World."

"We don't need training," Pearl insisted. "We helped with the rain dragon. And Ben did an excellent job feeding the kelpie."

"I think training is a good idea," Ben said, the empty fish bucket swinging from his hand.

Pearl waited, watching Dr. Woo's face. Would she say yes?

"I'm not in the habit of taking apprentices into the Imaginary World unless it's absolutely necessary," the doctor said. Pearl was about to groan with disappointment when Dr. Woo added, "But you may accompany me to the tenth floor, and we shall see what is going on."

That sounded far better than no. Pearl scampered up the stairs, her skinny legs carrying her two steps at a time. There was still a chance to change the doctor's mind about going to the Imaginary World. Pearl and Ben might not have to poke around in the sasquatch's nose after all!

It was a long trek up the stairs. Pearl had pointed out that they could use the elevator, but Dr. Woo had said that exercise was important. Ben was huffing and puffing at the halfway point. When they finally reached the tenth floor, they were greeted by the following sign:

FLOOR 10
OFF LIMITS
DO NOT ENTER
STAY OUT
THIS MEANS YOU

Because they had the doctor's permission, Pearl ignored the sign and pushed open the door.

A vast, empty room stretched before them. Yellow fairy dust covered the floor, remnants from the Portal, which was powered by the glittery stuff. Dr. Woo and the kids quickly crossed the room, passing a row of windows that offered a panoramic view of Buttonville. Town Hall towered above the rest of the buildings.

An old-fashioned telephone switchboard was set up along the far wall, its operator perched on a stool. "Howdy, y'aaaaall," Violet bleated with a wave. She wore a headset over her blond beehive hairdo. Her red dress was covered in white polka dots, and her hooves were painted to match. She was a satyress, which is a creature who is half human and half goat. She grabbed a handful of oats from a sack and stuffed them into her mouth. When she chewed, her little beard moved up and down. "How y'all doin'?"

"Fine," Pearl and Ben said.

"Well, I'm just plum tuckered ooooout." Oats flew

from her mouth. "I've been sitting here all morning, worrying myself into a tizzy. I am fluuuuustered."

"What are you worried about?" Ben asked.

"Did Mr. Tabby explain our current situation?" Dr. Woo asked her apprentices.

"He said that a human had been spotted in the Imaginary World," Pearl said.

"That is correct." Dr. Woo's voice remained calm. "Violet is worried that the man will try to leave the Imaginary World. And if he does, there's a chance he'll use our Portal." She leaned against the switchboard. "Is that why you summoned me? Has he been seen again?"

Violet swallowed. "Oh nooooo. It's something else entirely. But it's gosh darn difficult for me to make head or tail of it. You know how those unicorns are. They don't make one bit of seeeeense."

"Unicorns?" Pearl cried. "Really? I love unicorns!" Even Ben smiled because everyone knows that unicorns don't eat children.

"Is there a message?" Dr. Woo asked. But Violet

had stuck her head right into the sack. The only answer was muffled chewing sounds. Dr. Woo had to pull the oats away to get her attention. "Violet, what did the king say?"

"King?" Pearl could barely contain herself. She started to bounce around like a jumping bean. "Unicorns have a king? Does that mean they have a queen? Can I meet them?" Ben stepped away so Pearl wouldn't land on one of his feet.

"I wrote down exactly what he saaaaaid." Violet handed Dr. Woo a piece of paper. Pearl and Ben peeked around the doctor's arms to read the note.

THE BLESSING IS BROKEN.

"What does that mean?" Pearl asked.

"A blessing is a group of unicorns," Dr. Woo explained. "Only one blessing exists in the Imaginary World. If it is broken, one of its members must be missing."

"Hey, stop that," Ben complained. Violet had slid off her stool and was nibbling on his sleeve. He pulled it free. She bleated, then stuck her head back into the oats bag.

"Unicorns don't usually wander away from their own kind," Dr. Woo said. "The forest is full of dangers. If it's a very young unicorn, then it might have gotten lost. Which means..." Her arm fell to her side.

"What?" Ben asked.

Dr. Woo looked like she was in pain. She slowly crumpled the paper. Pearl's mind raced. What could happen to a unicorn if it got lost? What was waiting in the forest that might hurt it? A terrible thought occurred to Pearl. "Unicorns have horns," she said. "Is that what everyone is worried about? Is the human the same man who took the rain dragon's horn?"

Violet's head popped out of the bag, and she blinked rapidly.

For a long moment, no one spoke. Then Dr. Woo let the note fall to the floor. "Yes," she said. "Maximus Steele is on the prowl."

9

P earl tried to remember everything she and Ben had learned about Maximus Steele. He was a hunter, and he trapped the rain dragon in order to steal one of her horns. According to Dr. Woo, Mr. Steele was extremely dangerous, but she hadn't told them anything else.

"Is he mean enough to hurt a unicorn?" Pearl asked.

"He would do anything for a prized horn." Dr. Woo picked up the crumpled note and tossed it into a wastepaper basket. "But there's no time to discuss that right now. I must visit the unicorn king and find out what has happened."

"Good luck," Ben said.

"Please take us with you," Pearl pleaded. This was the opportunity of a lifetime. She had to go! "We can help."

"I don't think..." Dr. Woo paused. Then she pressed her fingertips together and gazed at Pearl. "In any other situation, I would be hesitant. Mr. Tabby has not yet trained you in certain procedures. But in the case of a unicorn, Pearl, you might be of great value."

"Really?" Pearl beamed.

"While the kelpie preferred Ben's scent, unicorns prefer the company of young girls. In fact, only a girl can summon a unicorn."

"Hey!" Ben cried. Violet had found the yellow knitted hat in his back pocket and was nibbling on the yarn. He pulled it free. "How come you keep eating my clothes?"

She blinked rapidly. "I can't help myself, little darlin'. I just love to eeeeeat."

"Goats like to eat everything," Pearl said. "I saw a show once where a goat was eating a tin can. Am I right?" She smiled, but then realized that Dr. Woo and Violet were looking at her as if she'd just said the most horrid thing in the world.

Violet put her hands on her wide hips and scowled. "I'm no goooooat," she said huffily. "I'm a satyress. Goats are simple, domesticated critters from the Known World. I am descended from a Greek demigod, not from a faaaaarm animal." She grabbed a bag of ivy and began chewing on a vine.

"Sorry," Pearl said. She hadn't meant to insult anyone.

Dr. Woo cleared her throat. "I must attend to the unicorns. Violet, while I'm collecting my supplies, please have the apprentices watch the Portal training movie." She began to walk toward the stairwell.

"We have to watch a training movie?" Pearl complained. "That sounds boring. Can't we just learn on the job? My dad says that's the best way to learn."

"Will we be back by three?" Ben called. "My grand-father wants me home because he's making brisket for dinner. It's his favorite."

"I will make every effort to return you by three o'clock," Dr. Woo said. Then she left the tenth floor, the door closing behind her.

Pearl poked Ben's arm. "If we're late, we won't have to go to Victoria's award ceremony. I'd rather feed sardines to that kelpie than watch someone put a crown on Victoria's big, bloated head."

Violet wiped a few bits of green leaf from her mouth, then motioned with her hand. "Follow me, little daaaaarlin's."

A side door opened into a room that looked exactly like a miniature theater. Six red velvet chairs sat in a row facing a white screen. The walls and ceiling were painted black. An old-fashioned projector stood in the back of the room.

"Wow," Ben said as he looked at the contraption. The film was wound onto one reel, which fed it through the projector, then onto a second reel. "This is really old."

"Have a seeeeeat," Violet said, her hooves *click-clack*ing as she walked to the projector.

Pearl and Ben chose the two middle seats. Even though the hospital theater was small, it was so much better than the one in Buttonville, where the seats leaked stuffing and the metal springs poked into your back. The old popcorn machine always overcooked the kernels so that you had to spit out the little burned bits. That was why the floor was crunchy and sticky at the same time.

Violet darkened the room, then switched on the projector. A beam of light shot through the lens and onto the screen.

"Should we take notes?" Ben asked. "Is there going to be a test?"

Pearl groaned. She hated tests. No matter how much time her teacher gave her to study, she always seemed to forget something.

"Y'all pay attention and there'll be no need for a teeeeest," Violet said as she left the room.

The movie began.

10

PORTAL TRAINING

The movie was black-and-white, and covered in dust and scratches. A whirling tornado appeared on the screen.

FAIRYLAND ENTERTAINMENT
Presents

**HOW TO BE SAFE
WHEN TRAVELING IN THE PORTAL**

Starring: Sasquatch

A narrator began to speak. The voice was high-pitched and squeaky.

> *"Hello and welcome. We here at the*
> *Portal have produced this film to*
> *help you prepare for interdimensional*
> *travel. Our safety record is better*
> *than bad, and we want to keep*
> *it that way."*

Better than bad? Pearl and Ben looked at each other.

The sasquatch appeared on-screen. It held a small suitcase and wore a fanny pack around its waist. The narrator's voice continued. . . .

*"Welcome, Mr. Passenger. I see that
you have packed for your trip. It is
important to be prepared in case
your visit runs longer than expected.
Extra underwear, a toothbrush, and a
container of water are all good to bring
should something go wrong and you get
stuck for a day or two, or a year."*

"A year?" Ben said. He sat up straight. "But I
have to be back by three."

*"Always double-check to make certain
you are carrying a vial of fairy dust. It
is the only way to summon the Portal
for the return trip."*

The sasquatch reached into its fanny pack and
pulled out a vial. It sparkled yellow.

"Very good. We will now instruct you in the correct way to enter the Portal."

The camera shot widened to show the sasquatch standing next to the swirling tornado. The wind rustled the ends of its fur.

"It is important to walk directly into the Portal. Do not run, skip, or jump, as this could create a disruption in the magnetic field, causing the Portal to hyperextend or collapse upon itself, wreaking havoc on the space-time continuum. Go ahead, Mr. Passenger. Please enter the Portal at a steady pace."

The sasquatch pointed to the tornado. The camera moved up and down, as if nodding. The sasquatch

shook its head. A hand holding a chocolate bar appeared from the side of the screen. Then it tossed the bar into the Portal. The sasquatch smiled and bounded into the wind.

Pearl and Ben had learned, during their sasquatch-catching adventure, that the furry beasts love chocolate.

The next scene showed the sasquatch standing in a calm space, wind swirling at the perimeter. It had set the suitcase at its feet and was happily eating the chocolate bar.

*"Once you are safely inside the Portal
and have given the captain your
destination, you will prepare for takeoff.
Most Known World beings experience
discomfort during travel because
Known World beings usually travel in
only three dimensions—up and down,
side to side, and back and forth."*

The room suddenly moved up and down, side to side, then back and forth. The sasquatch looked up from its eating and growled.

"The Portal, however, travels in all dimensions at once. Let us show you what we mean."

Suddenly, the sasquatch turned into a giant blur. When it came back into focus, all of its fur was sticking straight up and its suitcase had toppled over. After teetering from side to side, it bared all of its teeth and growled so loud that the camera shook. The sasquatch reached out and swatted at whoever was standing behind the camera. The screen went black.

Pearl frowned, remembering how she'd felt a bit queasy during her first ride. She didn't blame the sasquatch for getting mad.

The movie resumed. There were more instructions

about seat belts, oxygen masks, and not littering inside the Portal.

"This is a weird movie," Pearl said.

"It beats the one we had to watch in health class," Ben told her. "It was called *Your Changing Body*, and it was all about pimples and BO." Both he and Pearl shuddered.

The Portal appeared on-screen again, only this time it was empty except for the chocolate bar's wrapper and the suitcase on the floor.

> *"This brings us to the most important safety rule of all: Never leave the Portal until the captain gives the orders to disembark. There's no knowing where you'll end up."*

The next shot showed the sasquatch sitting at the very top of a snow-capped mountain, shivering.

"But as long as you have your vial of fairy dust, you'll be fine. Thank you for your attention, and we hope to see you in the Portal."

**THESE SAFETY TIPS
WERE BROUGHT TO YOU BY THE FAIRIES,
PRODUCERS OF THE ORIGINAL
PORTAL-POWERING DUST.**

The End

The film reel made a flapping sound as it spun around and around. Ben hurried to the projector and turned it off. "That movie made me feel worse," he said. "I mean, what happens if I fall out but you've got the vial? Or if you fall out but I've got it?"

Pearl considered this for a moment. "I guess we just have to make sure that we don't fall out." She'd been on dozens of rides at the Milkydale County Fair, including the Whirl-a-Tron, the Freaky Frisbee, and the Loop-de-Loop, and she'd never fallen off a single one. "Besides, we're not going alone like last time. Dr. Woo is coming with us, so we'll be safe."

"Y'all ready?" Violet asked, poking her head into the theater.

"Yes," Pearl said, jumping out of her seat.

"Y'all excited about your trip?"

"I'm definitely excited," Pearl said.

"I'm wondering..." Ben shuffled in place. "Has anyone ever actually fallen out of the Portal?"

"Don't you worry, little darlin'. Dr. Woo will take good care of yooooou."

Pearl noticed that Violet hadn't actually answered Ben's question. But that didn't stop her from wanting to go. She'd be sure to stand right in the middle.

Dr. Woo was waiting outside the theater, her medical bag in hand. Violet blinked rapidly. "I'd feel

a lot safer if Mr. Tabby were here," she said. "My nerves are all aquiiiiiver."

Dr. Woo patted Violet's shoulder. "Should there be any problems, Metalmouth is in the lobby."

After eating a handful of oats, Violet climbed onto her stool and pushed a large yellow button. A clap of thunder sounded in the distance. Then a roar closed in, as if the storm of the century were heading right for the hospital. A small tornado appeared in the center of the tenth floor, so tiny Pearl could hold it in her hand. Then it grew and grew, expanding until it touched the ceiling. Pearl and Ben stepped back as wind blew across their faces. Fairy dust lifted off the floor, turning the tornado yellow. Pearl wanted to plug her ears, the wind was so loud.

"Follow me," Dr. Woo ordered.

Even though this was the second time Pearl had stepped into a tornado, it still felt shocking. She expected the wind to pick her up and toss her around like a kite, but she walked right through and into the Portal. Ben followed, then stood next to her. It was too loud to talk, too loud for Pearl to tell him that everything would be okay. They wouldn't fall out. They wouldn't get lost. They'd have another wonderful adventure, and he'd be home in time for brisket dinner.

Pearl's ponytail came loose, and her hair whipped her neck and cheeks. A blurry image of Violet eating more ivy vines was the last thing she saw before everything went black.

11

DRAGONFLY HILL

A light flicked on above their heads. The tornado had widened, creating a calm space in its center. Pearl, Ben, and Dr. Woo stood on a solid floor, but the walls and ceiling were composed of swirling wind.

"Welcome to the Portal. This is your captain speaking." The high-pitched squeaky voice came from above. Pearl wondered what sort of creature that voice belonged to. She imagined a little grasshopper dressed in a captain's hat and uniform. "Destination, please."

"The Tangled Forest," Dr. Woo said as she set her bag next to her feet.

"Hello, Dr. Woo. Nice to see you again." The overhead light grew a bit brighter. "The runway on the south end of the Tangled Forest is currently under repair because of damage sustained during the migration of the giants. Will the northern runway suffice?"

"Yes, that will be fine."

Giants? Pearl mouthed at Ben, who was chewing on his lip again. He was probably imagining a herd of gigantic feet crushing everything in their path.

"Please fasten your seat belts," the captain said.

"There aren't any seat belts," Ben pointed out, "because there aren't any seats."

"We're having them reupholstered," Dr. Woo explained. "Interdimensional travel can be hard on fabric."

"Prepare for takeoff," the captain announced.

★97★

Takeoff was the part Pearl didn't like. The last time she traveled in the Portal, it had seemed like her insides were being scrambled. Was that how it felt on an airplane? Pearl had never been on one. In fact, she hadn't traveled much outside Buttonville.

A rumbling sound arose, like an engine revving its motor. Pearl braced herself, stiffening her legs and holding out her arms for balance. There were no windows in the wall of swirling wind, so she couldn't watch the houses grow smaller or the forest disappear as they headed into the clouds.

Suddenly, the Portal began to move in every direction at once, just like in the training movie. Maybe not having windows was a good idea, because Pearl wasn't sure if she was upside down, sideways, or inside out.

Ben groaned. Pearl closed her eyes. Just when she thought she might break into a million pieces, everything went still and quiet. She opened her eyes and wiped her sweaty palms on her basketball shorts. "Are we here?"

"Yes," Dr. Woo said.

Huge exhales of relief came from the apprentices. "Remind me not to eat a pancake sandwich before going on another Portal ride," Ben said, pressing a hand over his stomach.

Dr. Woo smoothed her hair, then turned and faced her apprentices. "Listen very carefully," she said in her calm, soft voice. "Before we step into the Imaginary World, there are a few important safety rules. Do not eat anything without checking with me first. Do not touch anything without checking with me first. And, the most important rule of all, do not make unnecessary noise."

"So we won't disturb the unicorns?" Pearl asked.

"So we won't disturb *other* things." The word *other* echoed throughout the Portal.

Ben scratched behind his ear. "Uh, what do you mean by that? We aren't going to run into another kelpie, are we?"

Dr. Woo picked up her medical bag. "One never knows."

An exit light illuminated. "Welcome to the Tangled Forest. We would like to thank you for flying with us today," the captain said. "We hope you will choose the Portal for your next interdimensional journey. Please refrain from pushing as you disembark."

"'One never knows'?" Ben whispered to Pearl as they followed the doctor. "She should know, don't you think? I mean, this is her *job*."

Pearl wasn't worried about the not-knowing. She didn't mind surprises, as long as they didn't want to eat her for breakfast. She stepped through the Portal's windy exit, hoping she wouldn't be disappointed. The Land of Rain hadn't been much to look at. Before landing there, Pearl had imagined purple trees, polka-dot clouds, and rainbows made of floating jelly beans. But it turned out to be a barren wasteland, parched and cracked as far as the eye could see. Would the Tangled Forest be nicer?

The wind swirled around and around. "I can't

see anything," Pearl complained, her hair flying. She took a few more steps.

Then the Portal disappeared, the wind blew away, and Pearl took a long, deep breath.

"Wow," she and Ben both said.

They stood on a hilltop. A carpet of lush lime-green grass sloped gently to the edge of a forest. Pearl turned in a slow circle. The forest surrounded the hill, spreading out in all directions. The trees were twice as tall as the ones in Buttonville. A buttery sun warmed Pearl's face. A light breeze kissed the blades of grass. "It's beautiful," she said.

"Keep your voice low," Dr. Woo warned. Then she gazed toward the forest, her eyes searching.

What is she looking for? Pearl wondered.

A butterfly flitted past Pearl's face and landed on Ben's head. "Don't move," she whispered, wanting to get a better look.

Ben froze. His eyes rolled upward. "Is something crawling in my hair?"

Pearl leaned close. The butterfly's wings were pink and sparkly, like the lipstick Mrs. Petal sometimes wore. "That's the prettiest butterfly I've ever seen," she whispered.

"It's not a butterfly," Dr. Woo said matter-of-factly. "Stand very still, Ben." She opened her medical bag and took out a magnifying lens, which she handed to Pearl. Pearl looked through the thick glass.

"Whoa. What is that?" The butterfly's body was green and fuzzy like a caterpillar's, but its tiny head looked exactly like a dragon's.

"It's a dragonfly," Dr. Woo explained. "But not like any you've ever seen. It's what's known as a hybrid creature—half one thing, half another."

"You mean it's half butterfly and half dragon?" Pearl asked. Dr. Woo nodded.

"Wait a minute," Ben said. "There's a dragon on my head? I don't want a dragon on my head. What if it spouts fire?"

"That is a possible outcome." Dr. Woo aimed her fingers and, with expert precision, flicked the critter from Ben's hair. It flew away. Then she sat in the grass, her legs crisscrossed, her hands resting in her lap. "We must wait for permission to enter the Tangled Forest. It is a sacred place."

"Who's going to give us permission?" Pearl asked, setting the magnifying lens back into the bag.

"The unicorn king."

Pearl shivered with excitement. This was really happening! She sat next to the doctor, her arms wrapped around her knees. After running his hands over his hair to make sure nothing else was crawling around, Ben also sat. A red dragonfly flitted past, then a blue one. A pink sparkly one hovered in front of Ben's nose. When he tried to wave it away, it shot a tiny flame at him. Pearl giggled.

"How long do we have to wait?" Ben asked, rubbing his nose.

Dr. Woo turned her face toward the sun and closed her eyes. "Unicorns cannot be rushed. They do everything at their own pace."

Pearl sighed. She hated waiting. Her legs felt twitchy, and she wanted to run down the hill and explore the forest. Maybe the unicorn king would let her ride on his back. A big stream of questions began to flow through her mind. But she remembered Dr. Woo's comment about quality, not quantity. So she focused on the one question that stood out above all the others.

"Dr. Woo, will you please tell us about Maximus Steele?"

Dr. Woo opened her eyes. "Yes," she said. "I think this is a good time to tell you his story."

12

Sunlight shimmered on Dr. Woo's black hair, glinting off stray specks of fairy dust. Her almond-shaped black eyes looked out over the Tangled Forest. Even with that scar on her face, Pearl thought she was the prettiest woman she'd ever seen. And definitely the most mysterious. She and Ben knew very little about her, only that she lived in Iceland before moving to Buttonville, and that she had the most amazing job in the world. They'd also learned that she'd met a dangerous man named Maximus Steele. Now she was going to tell her apprentices more about him.

The grass was quite comfortable—spongy and warm. Pearl scooted closer to the doctor so she wouldn't miss a word of the story. Ben pushed up the sleeves of his lab coat, equally eager to hear the tale.

Dr. Woo softly cleared her throat. As she spoke, she kept her voice quiet, continuing to watch the forest. "When I was about your age, I worked as an apprentice to my grandmother, Dr. Diamond Woo, one of the most respected veterinarians to care for Imaginary creatures. We'd moved to a new town, and I was going to school on weekdays and apprenticing on weekends. I was also on my school's soccer team and in the marching band, so you can imagine how busy I was."

"I love soccer," Pearl blurted so loudly that she startled a passing dragonfly. It squeaked with alarm and fluttered away. "Oops. Sorry." She brushed her loose hair from her eyes.

"Perhaps we can play a game sometime." Dr. Woo pulled a rubber band from her pocket, then proceeded to gather Pearl's hair into a ponytail. "Unfortunately, secret veterinarians often move from town to town to avoid being detected. Because of this, I didn't have many friends. And because I could never invite anyone to my house, I never had a best friend. That is, until I met Maximus." She turned and spoke directly to Ben. "He looked a bit like you in those days. When you stepped into my office that first time, I thought you were a ghost from my past."

"I don't believe in ghosts," Ben said.

"I don't blame you for not believing in them. They are very difficult to see, and in many cases, seeing *is* believing." She turned her focus back toward the forest. A few treetops rustled. Pearl sat up straight. Was something out there? She and Ben held their breath as more treetops rustled. When nothing appeared, Dr. Woo shifted position and continued her story.

"Max made me laugh. He was the class clown, always telling jokes and pulling silly pranks. We went to marching band practice together. He played the tuba, and I played the flute. We'd get in trouble because when we were laughing, we couldn't walk in a straight line. One day, he laughed so hard he fell right over and dented his tuba." Her mouth turned up slightly, forming a brief smile as she remembered this moment. Then her smile faded.

"His family was very poor, and they couldn't afford to buy a new tuba, so he was kicked out of marching band."

"That doesn't seem fair," Pearl said.

"Without marching band practice, Max didn't have anything to do," Dr. Woo told them. "Because he was my best friend, I persuaded my grandmother to make him an apprentice. I swore to her that he was a good person. I promised her that he could be trusted." She picked a blade of grass and ran it through her fingertips. "He never broke the contract of secrecy. But he showed signs of temptation, and that worried my grandmother."

"Temptation?" Ben asked.

"Max had been brought up always wanting for something," she explained. "He never had new clothes or nice shoes. His family got their food from the food bank, and he was often hungry. When he saw all that the Imaginary World had to offer, he began to scheme ways to get rich. He told me that we should take a few of the creatures and sell them to a zoo. Of course I refused. A Woo could never do such a thing.

One day, he put a fairy in his pocket and tried to bring it back through the Portal. My grandmother found out and fired him."

The breeze picked up, rustling branches. In the distance, a flock of giraffe birds took to the sky.

"We had to move, of course. Grandmother was afraid that Max would reveal our secrets. We left in the middle of the night. I was too angry to say goodbye. I had just started to feel at home, and because of him, I had to leave a soccer team, a marching band, *and* a best friend. He'd ruined everything." She paused. Pearl felt as if an eternity had passed before Dr. Woo started talking again. "The next time I saw him, I'd just graduated from university. We ran into each other at a conference. He'd become a famous animal collector and was giving a lecture on how to trap exotic creatures. He said he still wanted to be my friend. But what he really wanted was access to the Imaginary World."

Pearl remembered the giant trap that had been used to capture the rain dragon. "How did he get in?" she asked.

"I don't know."

"Is this why the unicorn blessing is broken?" Pearl asked. "Did Maximus Steele come here to take a horn?" She almost didn't want to know the answer.

"It's possible." The doctor's expression was heavy with concern. "A unicorn horn is the most coveted horn of all."

"Why?" Pearl asked.

"Because it contains magic."

"Really?" Ben shooed away another dragonfly. "What can it do?"

"When ground to a fine powder, a unicorn horn can cure illness and make poisoned water drinkable."

"Wow. That could help a lot of people," Ben said. "The water in Los Angeles isn't poisonous, but it tastes terrible."

"I don't understand something," Pearl said. "Why would he have to trap a unicorn to get a horn? I mean, couldn't he find one on a unicorn skeleton?"

"Once a unicorn dies, its body disappears. Nothing is left behind. So the only way to get a horn is to take it from a living unicorn."

Pearl pictured the big gaping wound that had been left on the rain dragon's head. How could someone do that to another living creature?

"Look," Ben said, pointing at the forest. A patch of trees swayed. Something was moving through the foliage, leaving a trail of rustling branches in its wake.

Dr. Woo got to her feet. "Don't say a word," she ordered.

Pearl and Ben stood, silently watching as the movement headed toward the forest's edge. Then a wondrous sight emerged.

Pearl nearly forgot how to breathe.

13

THE UNICORN KING

He wasn't wearing a crown, but by the way he held his head high, Pearl knew she was looking at the unicorn king.

He stood at the bottom of the hill, a blaze of white against the green forest background. He was as large as the draft horses Pearl had seen at the Milkydale County Fair. His neck and legs were thick with muscles, and his glossy mane looked like it was made of silk threads. His spiral horn sparkled as if it had been dipped in white glitter. He flared his nostrils and sniffed the air. Then he looked up at them and stomped his front hoof.

Dr. Woo turned to Pearl and Ben. "Remain here and keep still. Any sudden movement might spook him." She removed her creature calculator from her pocket and carefully walked down the slope.

Pearl pressed her shoulder against Ben's. "This is so amazing," she whispered.

"Unbelievable," he agreed.

Once Dr. Woo had reached the king, she placed her palms together and bowed. He dipped his head

in return. Then, holding her creature calculator, Dr. Woo began to speak, but the kids couldn't make out the words. The unicorn nodded, then raised his upper lip and neighed. Dr. Woo read from the calculator. "It must be translating," Ben said.

"I thought unicorns would talk, the way Metalmouth does." Pearl fiddled with one of the buttons on her lab coat. She could barely stand still.

The king snorted. Both he and Dr. Woo bowed, then he turned and disappeared into the forest. Pearl bounced on her toes as Dr. Woo walked back up the hill. "What's going on?" Pearl asked. "What did he say?"

"It's bad news, I'm afraid. The youngest member of the blessing is missing. She wandered into the darkest section of the forest, which is especially dangerous. The blessing is forbidden to enter that area, so they are unable to search for her."

"Why would she wander off?" Ben asked.

"Something made her curious," Dr. Woo said.

Pearl frowned. "Or *someone*."

Dr. Woo picked up her medical bag. "We must not jump to conclusions. A doctor must always assess the situation with logic. I have told the king that we will do our best. The Dark Forest awaits."

"Huh? Are you saying that we're going in there?" Ben asked. "If it's too dangerous for unicorns, isn't it too dangerous for people?"

"Ben Silverstein," Dr. Woo said patiently, "I will never force you to do something that makes you uncomfortable. You do not have to accompany us. You can stay here on the hill until we return. But, Pearl…" She placed her hand on Pearl's shoulder. "I need your help. The foal will only feel safe with a young girl. Will you go with me?"

"Yes, of course, I want to go with you," Pearl said, jutting out her chin. She was glad Dr. Woo hadn't listed all the dangers that lurked in the Dark Forest, or Pearl might have changed her mind.

So Dr. Woo and Pearl headed down the hill. Halfway, Pearl glanced back over her shoulder. Ben stood at the top, a big frown on his face, the breeze

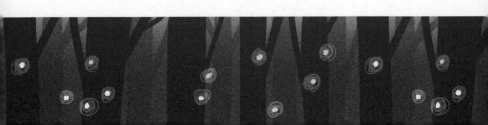

blowing the hem of his lab coat. It was too bad he wasn't going with them, but she understood. Ben didn't like dangerous stuff.

"Hey, wait!" he called, then started running down the hill. Pearl smiled as he caught up. "I want to help."

Dr. Woo stopped at the forest's edge, where the grass ended and thick undergrowth began. "Very well. But remember what I told you," she said with a serious tone. "Do not eat or touch anything without checking with me. Our plan is this: We make our way through the Tangled Forest until we reach the dark wall. We enter the Dark Forest to begin our search. And, finally, we evade predators and find the unicorn foal."

"Predators?" Ben asked.

Dr. Woo patted his shoulder. "Focus on the first goal, Ben, which is the dark wall. And be as quiet as possible." She gripped her bag.

Pearl took a deep breath. Quiet was not something that came easily to her.

Whoever had named the Tangled Forest chose well, for there was no path. The undergrowth of ferns and vines was knit as tightly as one of Aunt Gladys's blankets. How were they going to get through without a machete or a Weedwacker? Pearl wished she'd worn jeans, like Ben, so her legs would be protected from scratches. But then she stopped worrying because when Dr. Woo took a step, the branches and ferns moved aside, as if welcoming her.

"Whoa," Ben said.

As the doctor took another step, then another, the forest bowed, creating a narrow pathway. Dr. Woo motioned for her apprentices to follow. Pearl darted in front of Ben, but just as she took her first step, the undergrowth bent back into place, blocking the way.

Dr. Woo disappeared from sight.

14

THE POSITIVE PATH

"Hey," Pearl said. "What happened?" She tried moving the branches out of the way, but they wouldn't budge. She was about to holler for help when the doctor peered over the top of a shrub.

"Pearl? Why aren't you following?"

"I can't," she said. "The path disappeared."

"Ben, did you try?"

"No," Ben said. "Pearl went first."

"Go ahead and step forward," Dr. Woo told him.

With a shrug, he stepped in front of Pearl and—voilà—the undergrowth bowed and bent, moving aside to form a little path. "It's working again," he said. "Does this forest use some sort of motion detector? Maybe there's a glitch in the system." He started walking, his sneakers crunching twigs and dried leaves. "Our four-car garage back home had a problem with its motion detector. It nearly squashed our neighbor's cat." The forest continued to open until Ben reached the doctor. They both turned and looked at Pearl.

She stood in the grass, just outside the forest, her face clenched with puzzlement. Why had the plants blocked her but not Ben? "Come on," Ben urged.

Pearl took a step. The undergrowth snapped shut. *Huh?* She clenched her fists. *What is going on?*

Dr. Woo peeked over the shrub again. "I think I know what the problem is. The Tangled Forest will only welcome those who are pure of heart."

"I'm pure of heart. I'm totally pure of heart," Pearl insisted. She scratched her neck. "What does that mean, exactly?"

"It means you harbor no ill will."

"I don't harbor any ill will." She folded her arms

across her chest. "What does *that* mean, exactly?"

"Are you angry with someone?" Dr. Woo asked. "Do you wish for something bad to happen to anyone in particular?"

"No," Pearl blurted.

"What about Victoria?" Ben said, poking his face over the shrub. "You're mad at her, remember."

"I don't like her," Pearl said, tightening her arms. "But that doesn't mean I want something bad to happen to her." She looked down at her pink leprechaun shoes. She had tons of reasons not to like Victoria. Everybody in town thought Victoria was perfect. To make matters worse, that night she'd be getting a crown and a special party. She'd probably become the queen of Buttonville. "She doesn't deserve that crown," Pearl grumbled under her breath.

Dr. Woo nodded. "Close your eyes and clear your mind, Pearl. When we wish the best for others, then we make possible the best for ourselves."

Pearl closed her eyes. She tried very hard to

wish the best for Victoria. But when she imagined Victoria wearing that crown, she got a tight feeling in her stomach. *You can do this,* she told herself. *You can be happy for Victoria.* Pearl remembered how great she'd felt when Dr. Woo gave her the first certificate of merit. She'd read and reread it a hundred times that night. It had made her feel special. That was how Victoria would feel when she wore the crown. Everyone deserved to feel proud.

The undergrowth trembled, then bowed and moved aside. Pearl looked at the path with uncertainty. Would she be able to keep these positive thoughts, or would the trail close around her, leaving her stranded?

"Pearl?" Dr. Woo called.

"I'm coming."

They walked for a long while with Dr. Woo in the lead. The forest's dense canopy hid the sky from view, but light trickled between gaps in the leaves and branches. Ribbons of light cascaded down Dr. Woo's black hair. "Don't you think you should tell us about the dangers in the Dark Forest?" Ben asked. "So we can be prepared?"

"One thing at a time, Ben. First we must reach it."

He scratched his head. "How long will that take?"

"Patience is a better guide than haste," Dr. Woo replied.

"If the Tangled Forest won't allow anyone in who's not pure of heart, then how could Maximus Steele get in?" Pearl asked.

"He could enter the Dark Forest by way of the sky or through an underground tunnel. But we do not know that he has done such a thing. He may or may not be the cause of the foal's disappearance."

They walked quickly, Ben's sneakers crunching. The path continued to open a few paces ahead of Dr. Woo. "What are those things?" Ben asked quietly. He pointed to a swarm of glowing dots floating overhead.

"Fireflies," Dr. Woo said. "They stay inside the forest, where there's no wind. All it takes is a small breeze to extinguish them."

"They're actual *fire*flies?" Ben asked. Dr. Woo nodded. "Are they dangerous? Can I catch one?"

"That is doubtful," Dr. Woo said.

Ben reached up, but each time he tried to grab a fly, it darted away. He jumped, but missed again and again. "I want to see what they look like," he told Pearl.

She'd been wanting the same thing. Standing on tiptoe, she managed to grab one on her first try. Maybe being a head taller than Ben had given her an advantage.

The little bug felt like a warm kernel of popcorn. As Ben watched closely, Pearl slowly opened her fingers. The firefly sat in her palm. It looked like a fly, with a black body and black antennae, but its belly was on fire. Somehow it didn't burn Pearl's skin. "That's so weird," she said.

"Pearl?" Dr. Woo had stopped walking and was staring at her quizzically. "Please show me how you caught that."

The firefly flew away. Pearl looked around. Another fly circled above a fern. She walked over and grabbed it out of the air. "See," she said. "It's easy."

"It's not easy," Dr. Woo told her. "Fireflies can detect the slightest noise—that's what makes them nearly impossible to catch." Then she said something that made Pearl smile.

"It would appear that Cobblestone the leprechaun gave you a pair of silent slippers."

15

THE SLIPPERS' SECRET

Pearl had imagined all sorts of powers for her leprechaun shoes, but never this.

"Silent slippers?" She was so surprised she forgot all about having caught the second firefly. As her arms dropped to her sides, the little creature flew away. "You mean, they don't make any noise when I walk?"

Dr. Woo nodded. "If you can manage to make the rest of you quiet, then you can go anywhere in complete silence."

"The rest of me?" Pearl clamped a hand over her mouth. *Oh, right, the talking thing.*

"Do you realize what this means?" Ben asked. "You can sneak into places without getting caught. You're *so* lucky."

"This is a fortunate turn of events," Dr. Woo said. "Since you are the only one who can coax the unicorn foal out of hiding, I was going to ask you to enter the Dark Forest—alone. Of course, you could have refused." She crouched next to Pearl and touched one of the pink slippers. "But there's no need to worry. These will keep you safe from predators. What they cannot hear, they cannot catch."

"But they can still see me," Pearl said.

"Plants do not have eyes."

"Plants?" Ben spat out the word with surprise. "The predators are *plants*? That's good news. I was worried we'd run into another kelpie. Plants aren't a big deal, right? I mean, they can't chase after you."

Dr. Woo stood, then brushed dried leaves from her legs. "Plants are more dangerous because they have no brains and, thus, no intelligence. You cannot rationalize with them. You cannot bribe them or make a deal with them. They react by instinct alone. And when these particular plants hear someone coming, they attack."

"But they won't attack me, because they won't be able to hear me," Pearl said.

"Exactly. Cobblestone the leprechaun chose wisely when he gave you these slippers. Mine are quite different."

"You have leprechaun shoes?" Pearl asked.

"Yes. They allow me to walk on water, which comes in handy when I'm not wearing a bathing suit." Dr. Woo stepped aside. "Show us your slippers in action."

Pearl took some steps, then jumped up and down. She crushed sticks and leaves underfoot, but not a sound emerged.

"Can I borrow those for Halloween?" Ben asked.

"I could sneak up on people and totally scare them."

"Sure," Pearl said.

Something vibrated. Dr. Woo pulled out her creature calculator and read its screen. "I have good news and bad news. The good news is that I'm now able to pick up the foal's vital signs, which means she's not far from here. The bad news is that her heart rate is elevated—an indication that she's under stress."

"Do you think the plants are trying to hurt her?" Ben asked.

"Doubtful. Unicorns are also able to walk in silence, so the plants won't even know she's there. But something is scaring her."

"Or someone," Pearl grumbled.

They continued the journey with renewed urgency. The foliage moved aside, just like before, but after a few minutes the path ended at a wall of black. "We have reached the dark wall," Dr. Woo said. "It surrounds the Dark Forest."

Pearl tried to touch the wall, but it wasn't solid.

Her hand disappeared from view. She pulled it back into the dappled light. "You want me to go in there?"

"Yes," Dr. Woo said. "If Ben and I accompany you, the foal will not show herself. She will trust you and only you."

"Should I take the medical bag, too?"

"No. You will need both of your hands to be free. Unicorns do not like the dark, and you might need to carry her out."

"That's no problem," Pearl said. "I carry boxes at the Dollar Store all the time." She looked into the darkness. "How will I find my way back to you?"

"That is an example of a quality question," Dr. Woo said, but she offered no answer, which Pearl found very frustrating.

"You could use something to mark your path," Ben suggested. He took the yellow hat from his pocket. Thanks to Violet's nibbling, it had already begun to unwind. "You could tie pieces of yarn on the trees as you go."

"That's an excellent idea," Dr. Woo said.

Ben's plan reminded Pearl of a story her mother had read to her about a couple of kids who left a trail of bread crumbs when they walked into the woods. But the crumbs got eaten by birds, so the kids couldn't find their way back. "Wait," Pearl said. "Are there birds in the Dark Forest? Because some birds will steal yarn for their nests. I know because I have a nest collection."

Dr. Woo shook her head. "There are no birds in the Dark Forest."

"Okay." Pearl took the hat and tucked it into her lab coat pocket. "What plants am I watching out for?"

"They are called flesh-eaters. You can't miss them, because they grow in clumps, with enormous white flowers. They create a scent that each of us can't resist, but don't let it distract you. It's a trick."

Flesh-eaters? That sounded pretty bad.

Pearl fidgeted. She ran through the task at hand—go into the darkness, mark the trail with

bits of yarn, find the foal, carry it back to Dr. Woo—all while staying clear of flesh-eating plants. This was nothing like working at the Dollar Store, where the most dangerous items were the scissors.

But it was just another ordinary day in the Imaginary World.

"I have one last question," Pearl said. "How am I supposed to see where I'm going?"

Dr. Woo pointed overhead. Pearl reached up and grabbed a firefly. Then she grabbed two more. As she held them in her palm, light streamed between the cracks in her fingers.

"That should do it. Good luck." Dr. Woo patted Pearl's back. Then she added, "Try not to walk in circles. The Dark Forest can be very disorienting."

"Yeah, don't walk in circles," Ben said. "The shortest distance to something is a straight line. We learned that at math camp."

No one had said a word about Maximus Steele. *Maybe Dr. Woo was right*, Pearl thought. *We shouldn't jump to conclusions.* He could be a million miles

away, in some other land, bothering some other horned creature. There was no reason to assume he'd trapped the unicorn foal. Why worry if there was nothing to worry about? The truth would be revealed soon enough.

So, after taking a deep breath, Pearl stepped into the darkness.

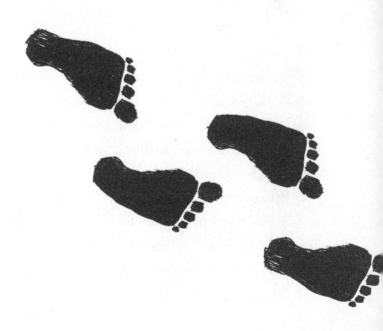

16

THE DARK FOREST

Pearl stood inside the Dark Forest. She wished Ben had come with her. They'd proved to be a good team. They'd caught a sasquatch together, they'd thwarted the Mulberrys together, they'd even gotten into trouble together.

But now she was alone.

She'd only known Ben for a week, but she was getting used to having him around. Too bad Cobblestone the leprechaun hadn't made another pair of silent slippers. If she ran into the little guy again, she'd ask him to make some. She'd wrap them in nice paper and give them to Ben for Christmas. Or for Hanukkah. Then she'd never again have to go into a creepy forest alone.

Pearl carefully opened her hand. The three fireflies were curled together, fast asleep, their little bellies flickering with flames. If she hadn't been on a lifesaving mission, she would have spent more time admiring their unusual design. But the foal needed her.

She closed her palm around the snoozing insects, turning her hand into a flashlight. She swept it to and fro so she could get a look at the terrain.

The Dark Forest wasn't tangled. Nothing grew on the ground—not a bit of moss, not a blade of grass. No gigantic white flowers, either, which was a huge relief. The trees were so tall that they reached up and out of the darkness, piercing the thick cloud ceiling like spears.

Pearl considered her options. Turning back would

take her to Dr. Woo and Ben. Right or left would take her along the Dark Forest's perimeter. Ben had said that the shortest distance to something was a straight line. So straight ahead she went.

The forest floor was mostly dirt, twigs, and dried leaves—crunchy stuff. But Pearl didn't have to worry about them. She could have been walking on air, for not a sound emerged from beneath her leprechaun shoes. Using her teeth, she tore a piece of yellow yarn from Ben's hat, then tied it around a branch. She repeated this process every twenty paces, counting exactly. Ben's idea was brilliant. Because yellow showed up well in the firefly light, it would be easy to retrace her steps.

As Pearl made her way through the forest, she thought about Dr. Woo's story. The doctor and Maximus Steele had been best friends *and* apprentices, just like Pearl and Ben. Weirder still, when Maximus was a boy, he'd looked like Ben. What strange coincidences. At some point, Maximus turned evil. There was no way Ben would turn evil.

He'd taken care of a wyvern hatchling, and he'd helped make a new horn for the rain dragon. He would never hurt a creature for its ivory, or fur pelt, or any reason. She'd bet her nest collection on that fact.

She bit off another piece of yarn. Pearl wasn't normally afraid of the dark. She didn't keep a nightlight in her bedroom, though that was mostly because the lamps on Main Street glowed outside her window all night long. But never in her life had she experienced such pitch-blackness. It began to feel smothering, like a heavy blanket pressed over her face. She walked faster. *Unicorn foal, where are you?*

One hundred and twenty paces in, she spotted something—a wisp of white hair hanging from a low branch. It was silky. It must have come from the foal's mane. Pearl was on the right track.

Just as she was tying another piece of yarn, a scent drifted out of the darkness. *How is that possible?* she wondered. It smelled exactly like a pancake

sandwich, with syrup and bacon. She loved those things! A feeling of longing washed over her, as if someone had dumped a bucket of homesickness on her head. She'd seen her parents just a few hours ago, but she missed them with all her heart. *Whatever you do, stomach, don't growl*, she thought. As she walked toward the scent, it filled her nostrils. She could practically taste the warm fluffiness.

That was when she saw the white flowers.

Flesh-eaters!

They grew in a clump, just as Dr. Woo had described. The huge white flowers reminded her of tulips with their petals closed tight. Pearl stood perfectly still, not even daring to blink. Luckily the little fireflies didn't snore. Pearl's mouth watered as the pancake scent grew stronger. Dr. Woo had said that flesh-eaters created different scents. How could they possibly know that Pearl liked pancakes? What would they smell like for Ben?

Giving the flowers a wide berth, Pearl walked around the clump. Not a single flesh-eater noticed.

There was no need to be afraid. *Not getting eaten is going to be easy*, she thought as she hurried away.

Forty more paces and she found another piece of white hair—a very good sign. She wanted to call out to the foal and let her know that help was coming. There were no flesh-eaters in sight. Maybe it would be okay. But that's when something flickered overhead, like a star in a black sky. She narrowed her eyes. The star grew larger. What was that? Was it floating downward? Toward her?

Dr. Woo had said to watch out for flesh-eaters. She hadn't mentioned anything else. Except for...

Maximus Steele!

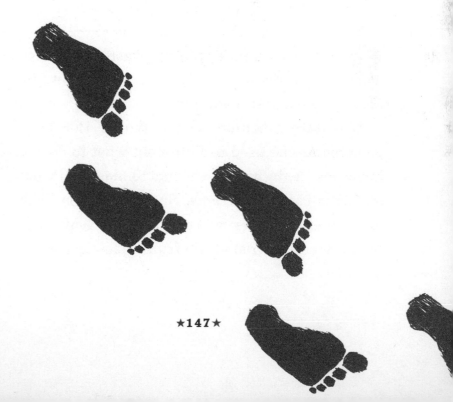

17

Pearl soon realized that she wasn't watching a star falling from the sky. It was a light, and someone was holding it.

She darted behind a tree trunk. Her heart pounded as she tried to figure out what to do. She knew, instinctively, that she had to hide from whatever was coming her way. She tucked her flashlight hand under her lab coat. Leaning against the tree, she peered around the trunk. The light moved steadily toward the ground. Tree bark pressed into Pearl's cheek. She wished Ben were standing next to her. Two against one was always better odds.

As it neared, the light grew too bright to look at. Pearl squinted, allowing her pupils to adjust. Then the light landed.

A man stood a few yards away. He held a small lamp in his right hand, a leather bag in his left. And strapped to his back was a huge moth the size of a dog! Together, they had glided down into the Dark Forest, as silent as a leaf falling from a tree.

Fear can make the entire body shake. It can turn the stomach to stone and cause thoughts to go all jumbled. So Pearl tried very hard not to be afraid. What she knew was this: Maximus Steele hunted creatures, not people. There was no reason why he'd hurt her. The flesh-eaters and the kelpie were much more dangerous.

But even so, she thought it would be best to remain hidden.

The man set the lamp and the bag on the ground. Then he unstrapped the moth but kept it tethered to a rope, which he tied around a tree. The moth panted with its furry mouth. Its wings went limp, falling on the ground like crumpled sheets. The lantern's glow illuminated the man's body, which was tall and thin. His pants were tucked into a pair of boots, and a knife hung from his belt. Because a pith helmet shaded his face, she couldn't get a good look at his features. He crouched, then removed something from his backpack. Lantern light reflected off the object's metallic surface. Pearl clenched her jaw. It was the same kind of trap Maximus Steele had used to catch the rain dragon, only much smaller. He set it on the ground.

Dr. Woo's story swept through Pearl's mind—images of a boy playing the tuba, telling jokes, laughing. Now he was sneaking through a forest, laying a trap to catch a unicorn. Pearl wanted to tell him to stop. She wanted to free the poor, tired moth. Maximus Steele was pure evil!

Turn around, she thought, hoping to see his face so she'd know him if she ever ran into him again. But he kept his back to her as he pulled open the sharp teeth of the trap. It clicked into place, like the jaws of a shark waiting to feed.

The sound echoed through the forest.

Uh-oh!

A rumbling arose in the distance. With calm and steady hands, Maximus untied the moth and strapped it to his back. Then he picked up the lantern and bag. Without a word, he jabbed the moth with his elbow. It unfurled its wings and began to flap gracefully, silently carrying them upward until they vanished into the cloud ceiling.

The rumbling grew louder. Holding out her flashlight hand, Pearl hurried to the trap. The man's initials—MS—were etched into the metal. With her free hand, she picked up a fallen branch and shoved it into the open jaw. As the razor-sharp teeth snapped around the wood, a *clang* rang out. Would Maximus return, thinking he'd caught his prey?

The forest floor trembled as the rumbling closed in. Pearl didn't know in which direction to run. Was there time to climb one of the trees? She spun around. White shapes charged toward her, their petals snapping wildly. The flesh-eaters had pulled their roots from the ground! They were using them like legs! Just in time, Pearl leaped behind a tree. The carnivorous plants ran straight for the trap—the source of the noise.

Then they attacked.

They flung it around and stomped on it until there was nothing left but mangled bits of metal. Then, as the forest grew silent once again, they tucked their roots back into the ground, closed their petals, and waited for their next meal.

This place was getting creepier by the minute! Pearl took off, running deeper and deeper into the forest, forgetting about leaving a trail of yarn. When her side began to ache, she stopped. There'd been no more white hair, no signs at all that the foal had come this way.

Pearl sank onto a rock, trying to catch her breath. Had she failed? Would Maximus find the lost unicorn before she did? Tears stung the corners of her eyes. She wanted to go back, but she couldn't leave the foal all alone in this evil place. Poor little thing.

How could she call out to it without making any noise? She couldn't whistle or snap her fingers. The slightest sound would alert those nasty plants. And possibly Maximus Steele, too. How could Pearl summon the unicorn?

Then she had an interesting idea. The path had opened because she'd gotten rid of her negative thoughts. Maybe in this darkest of dark places, the unicorn's path would also open with positive thoughts. It was worth a shot. Pearl closed her eyes and cleared all the scary pictures from her mind. She conjured the things that made her feel warm and safe—fluffy pancakes, bird nests, leprechaun slippers, hot cocoa, her parents tucking her in at night.

A soft, warm puff of air blew across her hand.

Slowly, she opened her eyes.

18

A PAIR OF CROWNS

Before Dr. Woo moved to Buttonville, there were three moments in Pearl's life that she loved better than any others—the first time she found a bird nest, the first time she pulled back her pillow to discover that the tooth fairy had visited, and the first time she rode a pony.

This moment topped them all.

The puff of air that touched Pearl's hand came from the soft muzzle of the unicorn foal.

She stood so close that Pearl could have petted

her silky white mane and touched her spiral horn. But Pearl didn't. She sat very still, afraid to scare the little creature, who was only a couple of feet tall.

The unicorn's hind legs trembled. That was when Pearl noticed that she held her right front hoof slightly above the ground. She'd been injured. *Don't be scared*, Pearl wanted to say. *Dr. Woo will help*

you. Pearl held out her hand, the way you do with a dog you don't know. The foal smelled her, then bent her head as the unicorn king had bent his. Pearl bowed in return. She could have sat there all day, gazing upon this beautiful creature. But Maximus Steele wanted that horn, and there was no way Pearl was going to let him have it!

Slowly, Pearl stood, then, keeping her hand closed around the fireflies, she slid her arms under the unicorn's belly and lifted. She smiled, happy to discover that the foal wasn't any heavier than a basket of laundry.

With silent speed, she began to retrace her steps—at least, that's what she hoped. But as she searched for yellow yarn, she found none. *Don't panic*, she told herself, instinct pulling her forward. She was certain she'd come this way, certain she'd find a piece of yarn. Never slowing her pace, Pearl ran and ran. The unicorn was warm against her chest, its heart beating as fast as a bird's. Pearl wanted to tell the little creature that everything would be okay, but how could she be sure? What if

they were lost? What if the giant moth dove down from the clouds and carried the foal away?

Doubt filled Pearl's mind. Her arms began to throb. *Not much farther. Keep going.* Just as she thought she might drop the unicorn, a voice called from the darkness. "Pearl! We can see the bobbing light. We're over here!"

The words vibrated through the darkness. Although Pearl was happy to hear Ben's voice, she knew the loud sound would bring danger. Roots ripped from the ground, and a stomping arose. Ben's voice had woken the flesh-eaters! Though she had little strength left, Pearl took a huge breath and pumped her legs. There'd been no flesh on the metal trap, but there was plenty to be found on a girl and a unicorn. Ben was near. His voice was her path. "Pearl!"

A blaze of light hit Pearl's eyes as she burst into the Tangled Forest. "Get back!" Dr. Woo warned, stepping between Pearl and the dark wall. A flesh-eater poked out of the darkness, its petals snapping like jaws. Dr. Woo aimed a spray bottle, and a

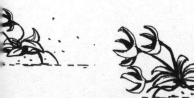

★160★

stream of liquid shot at the flower. The petals began to sizzle, and the plant retreated with a hissing sound. For a moment, all was quiet.

Except for Pearl, who was breathing like a racehorse. "You've got spray that kills flesh-eaters?" she asked. "How come you didn't give me some?"

"You are not authorized to use this particular serum without further safety training." Dr. Woo took the foal and laid her on the ground.

Ben looked at Pearl. "You okay?"

"Yes," she said. "You saved me. I was lost, but then I heard your voice." She hugged him so hard he groaned.

"You're…squeezing…me."

"Sorry." She let him go. Pearl needed to catch her breath, but she also wanted to tell Dr. Woo everything. "He's in there. Maximus Steele. I saw him. He had a moth strapped to his back, and he flew in and laid a trap."

"That is terrible news that requires our attention," Dr. Woo said. "But right now we must focus on our patient. That is always our first priority."

Pearl sat beside the medical bag, watching as Dr. Woo took the foal's temperature and felt for broken bones. While the doctor wrapped a bandage around the foal's ankle, Ben picked up the spray bottle and read the label. "'Nasty Weed Repellent.'"

"*Nasty* is not a nasty-enough word," Pearl said with a shudder. She'd never again complain about having to pull weeds out of the alley behind the Dollar Store. Dandelions seemed like diamonds compared to the flesh-eaters.

Ben set the bottle back in the bag, then his eyes widened. "Look."

Pearl didn't know what to expect. Since she and Ben met Dr. Woo and became her apprentices, nothing had been ordinary. Was Ben staring at another carnivorous plant or a swarm of fire-breathing dragonflies? Were the giants migrating in their direction?

She swiveled around and squealed with joy. The unicorn king was prancing down the path. Pearl scrambled to her feet, as did Dr. Woo. Everyone bowed. With the creature calculator in hand, the doctor spoke. "The foal's ankle is sprained, but it will heal in a few weeks' time. She's dehydrated and needs her mother's milk. Other than that, she'll be just fine."

The unicorn king touched his nose to the foal's nose. Then he looked at Dr. Woo and neighed. Dr. Woo read the calculator's screen. "There is no need to thank me, Your Highness. My apprentice Pearl is the one who found your daughter."

"His daughter?" Pearl asked. She'd saved *a princess*? "Wow!"

Then she grabbed Ben's sleeve and pulled him close. "Ben helped, too. I was lost, and he's the reason we found our way out of the Dark Forest." Ben's cheeks turned red.

The unicorn king neighed again. Dr. Woo read the screen. "He thanks you both and says that you are to become members of his blessing."

"Really?" Pearl asked.

"Indeed. It is a huge honor." Dr. Woo slipped the calculator into her pocket and removed a pair of scissors from her bag. The king bowed, and Dr. Woo snipped two thin strands of hair from his mane. Then she removed Pearl's ponytail holder. Pearl's hair fell to her shoulders. Dr. Woo touched the top of the unicorn strand to the middle part in Pearl's hair. Pearl felt a tickling sensation.

"It's attaching itself," Ben said with a gasp.

Though Pearl couldn't see it, the strand now looked as if it had grown right out of her head. The king's white unicorn hair blended with Pearl's blond human hair.

Then Dr. Woo tucked the second, shorter strand between layers of Ben's hair. "It tickles," he said. Pearl watched as the strand attached itself to Ben's head.

"It's hidden," she assured him. "No one will see it."

"Weird," Ben said as he touched his hair.

Pearl touched her hair, too. "What does this mean?"

Dr. Woo did not ignore this question. She answered it with her head held high, her voice full of pride. "It means, Pearl Petal and Benjamin Silverstein, that you are now members of the Order of the Unicorn. And those are your crowns."

19

A DOCTOR'S DUTY

One thing is certain about travel—the coming-back-home part is never as exciting as the getting-there part. Which is why Pearl didn't skip into the Portal with a huge grin on her face. And when Dr. Woo told the captain that their destination was Buttonville, Pearl's sigh was so long it could have inflated a balloon. She was sad to leave. The only unicorn back home was the tiny plastic one inside her Pony Parade board game.

Pearl longed to stay in the Tangled Forest. As a new member of the blessing, she wanted to spend time with the unicorn princess. Get to know her. Do some unicorn-y things, whatever those might be.

But alas, a minute later, her hair a tousled mess after the Portal ride, she stood alongside Ben and Dr. Woo on the tenth floor of the hospital. As her insides settled, the Portal disappeared, and the yellow fairy dust drifted to the floor.

Violet wasn't there to greet them. A note taped to her switchboard read:

SNACK BREAK
BACK IN 5.

"Can I visit the unicorn princess again?" Pearl asked as she and Ben followed the doctor to the stairwell.

"Visiting is not something we do, I'm afraid," Dr. Woo told her. "Human interaction in the Imaginary

World must be kept to a minimum. Therefore, we only travel when duty calls."

"What about Maximus Steele?" Ben asked as they stepped into the stairwell. "He's not supposed to be there. How'd he get in?"

An excellent question, Pearl thought, and one she wished she'd asked.

"The fairies who supply the dust that powers the Portal have an exclusive contract with my family. It has been this way for centuries. One human doctor, one contract. How Max got inside is a mystery." She started down the stairs, her steps quick and graceful.

"He took the rain dragon's horn," Pearl said, keeping pace beside the doctor. "And now he wants a unicorn's horn. How can we stop him? Are there police in the Imaginary World? My aunt Milly would be happy to go and arrest him."

"The laws in the Imaginary World are not the same as ours," Dr. Woo explained. They'd wound down the staircase, past floors nine, eight, and seven. "We are not supposed to interfere. I sprayed the flesh-eater out of necessity, but that was only because you are my apprentice and I am responsible for your safety. You needed my protection."

This didn't seem right to Pearl. "But…" They passed floor six. "But Maximus Steele is a human, like us. How can the creatures protect themselves from him?"

The doctor didn't answer this question. She quickened her pace. When they reached the second-floor landing, she opened the door and headed down the hall. Pearl and Ben soon found themselves in the familiar room that was Dr. Woo's office. As usual, it was crowded with crates and odd things, like giant bones, rainbow feathers, and jars of dead insects.

Dr. Woo set the medical bag on the floor, then stood in front of her office window, staring out over Button Lake. Her hands on her hips, she said nothing for a very long time. Pearl and Ben watched, waiting for her to make sense of the situation. Hoping she'd know how to fix it.

Finally, she turned around, her expression stormy. "My duty as a doctor is clear. I give medical care to Imaginary creatures, whether they are deadly like the kelpie or peaceful like the unicorn. I have never strayed from that responsibility. I am not meant to interfere in any other way."

Pearl imagined the unicorn foal and her beautiful horn. She remembered the gleaming teeth of Maximus Steele's trap. Her heart felt as heavy as a brick. How could Dr. Woo not do anything?

"However..." The doctor folded her hands and her dark eyes flashed. "Unicorns are special. And they're particularly special to me. So it would appear that I have a new duty. To find and capture Max and return him to this world."

"Yay!" Pearl and Ben cried.

Dr. Woo didn't smile. She sank into her desk chair. Then she pulled two pieces of paper from a drawer and wrote on them. "You have each earned a certificate of merit in the art of Saving a Unicorn Foal." She handed the certificates to Pearl and Ben.

"Thanks," they both said.

She nodded. "You may go now," she said, her voice heavy with exhaustion.

"Guess we'd better trim those nose hairs," Ben said after tucking his certificate into his pocket.

"Yeah, okay," Pearl grumbled. She turned to leave, but one more question needed to be asked. "Dr. Woo? Why are the unicorns special to you?"

With her four-fingered hand, Dr. Woo pulled back her hair, revealing a silky strand of white.

20

WORM TROUBLE

There are few places more disgusting than the interior of a sasquatch's nose. Not only did hair grow inside, but all sorts of things got stuck up there.

"Gross! Is that a booger?" Pearl asked.

"No," Ben said, examining the item. "I think it's a caterpillar."

The sasquatch didn't seem to mind. Pearl had found a chocolate bar in the Staff Room, so the stinky creature was perfectly content to sit and munch. The kids worked as fast as they could, snipping, picking, and trimming.

"Don't do that," Pearl scolded as the sasquatch stuck the candy wrapper up one of its nostrils.

It was a gooey situation, one that neither apprentice wanted to repeat. Relieved that they'd finished the task, they bid the sasquatch good-bye, then left in a hurry.

Once downstairs, Pearl and Ben returned the clippers to the Supply Closet, dumped their lab coats into the laundry bin, and washed their hands in the Staff Room. What remained of Ben's yellow hat was a mangled mess, so Pearl threw it away. "You can get another one from Aunt Gladys. She's got hundreds of them."

"Uh, thanks," Ben said, though he didn't sound very thrilled.

They punched their time cards and thumbtacked them to the OFF DUTY side of the bulletin board. Ben checked his watch. They had a few minutes to play fetch with Metalmouth and to fill him in on their latest adventure. As the dragon bounded after the yellow tennis ball, the lobby walls vibrated, loosening flakes of paint. His tail kept smacking the elevator button, sending the doors into a repeated rhythm of open and close. Pearl had to squeeze into the corner to keep from getting squashed. When the kids told Metalmouth about Maximus Steele, he dropped the ball and flattened his ears. "I don't like him. He's mean."

Pearl was expected back at the Dollar Store to do her afternoon chores. And Ben had agreed to help his grandfather with the brisket. "See ya Monday," Pearl said as Ben handed the tennis ball back to the dragon.

Metalmouth's tail *thwapp*ed. "Can we play fetch again then? Huh? Can we?"

"Sure," Ben told him. "I'd like that."

After the dead bolts slid into place, Pearl and Ben raced down the steps and across the overgrown lawn. They couldn't use the gate, since it was locked. Even though Metalmouth had the key ring, there was no way he could step outside, into the open, where everyone could see him. So they climbed over a rusty section of fence that they used for such purposes and landed on the sidewalk. The afternoon was sunny, the sky bright blue. No bread crumbs or

bits of yellow yarn were needed to guide them home. Pearl knew the streets so well she could have found her way blindfolded.

"Guess I'll see you tonight at Victoria's ceremony," Pearl said, her certificate of merit rolled in her hand.

"Yeah, guess so."

"I'm glad Dr. Woo is going to find Maximus Steele."

"Me too."

But then Pearl frowned. If Maximus wasn't allowed in the Imaginary World, did that mean he would come back to the Known World and start hunting the animals here? Maybe Dr. Woo could help him get a regular job—but not at the Dollar Store! No way would she work with someone who'd tried to hurt a unicorn!

"What are we going to tell people if they notice the unicorn mane in our hair?" She touched the silky strand, then pulled her hair back into a ponytail. "You better come up with a good story."

Ben smiled. "No problem."

They headed down Fir Street, then turned right onto Main Street, where they bumped into Mrs. Mulberry. Had she been waiting for them? She held a box.

"It arrived," she announced happily. The yellow shipping label read:

COMPOST WORMS
SPECIAL OVERNIGHT DELIVERY

Pearl frowned. "You got them already?"

"Yes, indeed." Mrs. Mulberry opened the box. Inside, a tangle of red worms glistened on a bed of wet dirt. But one worm lay in the corner, barely moving. "Looky, looky, this one's not doing so well." She smiled as if she'd found gold in a river, or a ruby in her ice cream.

Pearl and Ben exchanged nervous looks. Then they leaned closed. A tiny sound emerged from the worm. Was it possible? Had it actually...*coughed*?

"I've got a sick worm. That means I can make an appointment at the hospital." Mrs. Mulberry threw her head back and laughed with glee. "Now Dr. Woo has to see me!"

Drat!

CERTIFICATE OF MERIT
BEN SILVERSTEIN
IS HEREBY SKILLED IN THE ART OF
SAVING A UNICORN FOAL

CERTIFICATE OF MERIT
PEARL PETAL
IS HEREBY SKILLED IN THE ART OF
SAVING A UNICORN FOAL

PUT YOUR IMAGINATION
⚊ TO THE TEST ⚊

The following section contains writing, art, and science activities that will help readers discover more about the mythological creatures featured in this book.

These activities are designed for the home and the classroom. Enjoy doing them on your own or with friends!

CREATURE CONNECTION
★ *Unicorn* ★

The unicorn is one of the best-known creatures from mythology. It became very popular during the medieval period in European history—a time when kings, queens, and nobles ruled the land. Pieces of art from this age show the unicorn as a smallish white horse with a goat's beard, a lion's tail, and a pointed spiral horn in the center of its forehead.

Unicorns are symbols of purity and grace. During the medieval period, it was widely believed that these creatures actually existed. Legend said, however, that a unicorn would only show itself to a maiden—a young girl. If the maiden sat quietly, the unicorn would lay its head on her lap and fall asleep.

The unicorn's spiral horn was believed to be magical. If ground into dust, it could be sprinkled

into poisoned water, making the water drinkable. Poisoning was a real worry in those days, especially for members of a royal family. So hunters, hoping to get rich, tried to find the shy unicorn. They hired young girls, hoping to coax the creature from the forest.

Viking traders figured out another way to get rich. They came to Europe, carrying what they said were unicorn horns, also called alicorns. They sold them for more than double their weight in gold. It was a very profitable business. The Throne of Denmark is said to be made of unicorn horns. Even Queen Elizabeth I bought one. Crafty merchants ground these horns into powder and sold it as a medicine that could cure everything. Special cups were carved from alicorns and given to kings and queens to keep them from being poisoned.

We can look back on this period of time and laugh because we know that unicorns were made-up creatures and that the alicorns were actually narwhal tusks. Those Vikings were pretty clever.

Other cultures had similar unicorn-like creatures in their stories. The Chinese qilin had the body of a deer, the head of a lion, and a long horn in its forehead. It was said to be a good omen and thought to appear with the arrival and the passing of a great leader. The Japanese version was called the kirin.

The famous explorer Marco Polo wrote that he saw a real unicorn, but he described it as ugly, with dark buffalo hair and a large black horn, wallowing in the mud. What he actually described was a rhinoceros.

In 1663, a German mayor named Otto Von Guericke took the bones of a woolly rhinoceros, the bones of a mammoth, and the horn of a narwhal, and created a skeleton. Then he told everyone it was a unicorn. People traveled from far and wide to see this amazing find. Are you laughing again? I wonder what silly things we believe today that will make people laugh in the future!

STORY IDEA

You are a Viking and you've anchored your ship off the coast of England. You've rowed into a town, carrying a bag of narwhal horns. You want to trade them for gold coins. How are you going to convince the townsfolk that they are actually unicorn horns? What would you say? How could you prove it?

ART IDEA

According to legend, alicorn powder is a very powerful, magical medicine. Pretend you own a company that is trying to sell the powder. Draw a picture of your product. Does it come in a box, a jar, or a tube? What does the label look like? What information will you put on the package to persuade people to buy it? Look at some of the boxes in your pantry for ideas.

CREATURE CONNECTION
⋆ *Kelpie* ⋆

Creatures that are half horse are quite common in the mythologies of the world.

The ancient Greeks had stories about a half horse–half serpent called a hippocamp, which means "sea horse" in Greek. The chariot of Poseidon—the god of the ocean—was pulled by hippocamps. The Greeks also created centaurs, half horse–half human, and Pegasus, half horse–half bird.

The kelpie, half horse–half sea serpent, comes from Celtic folklore. The Celtic people lived in the regions we now call Ireland and Scotland. Horse in the front, sea serpent in the back, it lives in rivers and lakes, preferring areas where the water is turbulent. The kelpie is black or blackish green. It has a mane like a horse's, but its skin is said to be smooth like a seal's, and as cold as death.

Unlike the shy unicorn, the kelpie is not a peaceful creature. In fact, it is the exact opposite. While swimming below the water, it pokes its eyes just above the surface, waiting for victims to pass by. Because it is a shape-shifter, it can change its fins into legs and walk onto land. If someone wants to cross the river or lake, it will offer to give that person a ride. After the unsuspecting victim climbs onto the kelpie's back, the kelpie carries him into the water and...gobbles him up. The very worst part of all—kelpies are said to prefer the tender flesh of children. Creepy!

Why were stories told about such a terrible creature? Well, we all know that a fast-flowing river is dangerous. The same can be said about a deep lake, especially if you can't swim. This story was probably created by parents as a way to keep their children safe. Stay away from the water or the child-eating kelpie will get you!

So, if you ever encounter a dark horse and it offers you a ride across the water, there's one way you can tell if it's a real horse or a kelpie—a kelpie's mane never stops dripping.

STORY IDEAS

Imagine that you're going to the river to do some fishing. You see a horse talking to a little girl. The horse bends its front legs, offering the girl a ride. She's just about to climb on. But you know something that the girl doesn't know. How do you save her?

★ ★ ★ ★ ★

What is your opinion? Do you think all creatures deserve to be helped, even if they are harmful to us? Are there any exceptions?

SCIENCE CONNECTION
★ *What Are Horns?* ★

Horns, tusks, and antlers might all stick out of an animal's head, but they are very different things.

Tusks are teeth that keep growing and growing and growing. Tusks are made of ivory, which has been a precious material throughout human history. Therefore, the animals that grow tusks are often hunted, even when hunting them is against the law. Poachers, people who hunt illegally, are the worst enemy to animals that grow ivory tusks. These animals include walrus, elephants, warthogs, and narwhals. Yep, that's right. A narwhal actually grows a tusk, even though it looks like a horn.

Antlers are large, branching growths found only on members of the deer species. They grow in pairs and are covered with soft, velvety skin. When the antlers reach full size, they die and fall off. Then a new pair grows.

So what exactly are horns?

Horns are hard growths that come out of the head but are permanent, which means they don't fall off. They are living bones, and just like other bones, they don't regrow. Horns are found on cattle, sheep, goats, and even giraffes. Most horned animals have a pair, but some sheep have multiple horns.

Why do animals grow horns? One reason is for defense. Predators can be fought with sharp jabs. Territory can be defended with swift blows. Horns can also be used as tools for rooting in the soil to dig up food, and for stripping edible bark from trees. One of the most important reasons for horns is that males use them to attract females. This is called courtship. While a human male might put on cologne and a fancy suit to attract a lady's attention, the male antelope struts around, showing off his horns. *Look at my horns! Aren't they pretty?*

While we don't grow horns, we've sure found plenty of ways to use them. We transform them into

musical instruments, knives, and buttons. We drink out of them and carry gunpowder in them. The Chinese use antelope horn in medicine, too!

ART IDEA

You can make your own antler with a few simple and inexpensive items. Here's what you'll need:

a small branch from a shrub or tree
air-drying clay
a piece of sandpaper
some white acrylic paint
a paintbrush

First, find a small branch that is forked like an antler. Remove any bits of moss. Then cover the branch with a thin layer of clay. Allow it to dry fully for a day or two. Sand it smooth. Then paint the branch white.

It's not a real antler, but it sure looks like one!

HISTORY CONNECTION
★ *How Bad Is Poaching?* ★

Poaching is not a fun topic to write or read about. It can be very upsetting, but since we all share this planet, it's a subject we should understand.

Hunting is a legal activity. It is done at certain times of the year, on appointed lands, with weapons that have been approved for such purposes.

Poaching is illegal. It is the act of taking, selling, possessing, or killing protected animals. It is one of the most serious threats to animal survival. When Maximus Steele goes to the Imaginary World to take a horn, he is a poacher.

Poaching can be as simple as dropping a crab pot into the water and collecting crabs to eat during a month when crabbing is not allowed. Off-season crabbing is harmful because there are certain times of the year when crabs mate and produce young crabs. Taking too many females can reduce the number of crabs in the next year. This is an example

of how the actions of poachers can affect the food supply at large.

All sorts of creatures are the victims of poaching. Walrus and elephants are killed for their tusks. As we learned in the last section, a tusk is made of ivory, which can be worth a lot of money on the black market. The black market is a place where illegal items are sold.

Many creatures are endangered, which means they might go extinct in our lifetime. Poachers don't seem to care. There is money to be made, so they go after animals such as black rhinos, mountain gorillas, lions, and mountain zebras, just to name a few.

What can we do? We can make sure that if we buy a pet, we never buy an exotic creature that has been taken from the wild. We can also make sure that we never buy ivory.

If you would like to learn more about poaching and ways you can help prevent this crime, ask your teacher or parent to search online for one of the many organizations dedicated to protecting endangered species.

CREATIVITY CONNECTION
★ *Draw a Hybrid Creature* ★

Now for something fun!

A hybrid creature is made up of two or more creatures. In this book, Pearl and Ben met a kelpie, which is part horse and part sea serpent.

It's your turn to create your own hybrid creature. If you're having trouble thinking of some ideas, use this helpful list. Or come up with something totally different. It's up to you!

Combine a creature from Column A with a creature from Column B. Draw a picture of your creature. Give your creature a name.

COLUMN A	COLUMN B
Giraffe	*Goldfish*
Panda	*Spider*
Wolf	*Snake*
Cat	*Butterfly*
Pig	*Turtle*
Mouse	*Caterpillar*
Rabbit	*Bumblebee*
Dog	*Shark*
Owl	*Octopus*
Dinosaur	*Hummingbird*

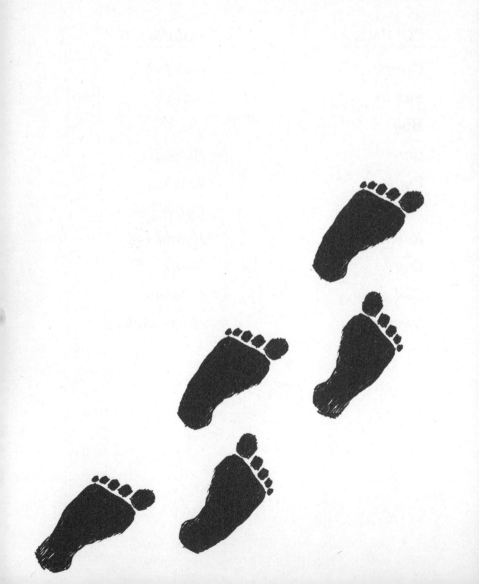

DON'T MISS THE NEXT ADVENTURE

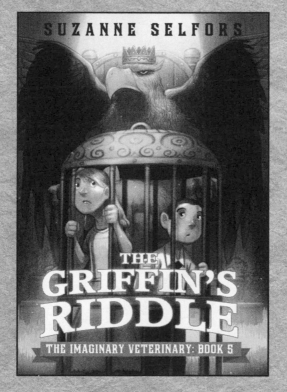

Turn the page for a sneak peek!

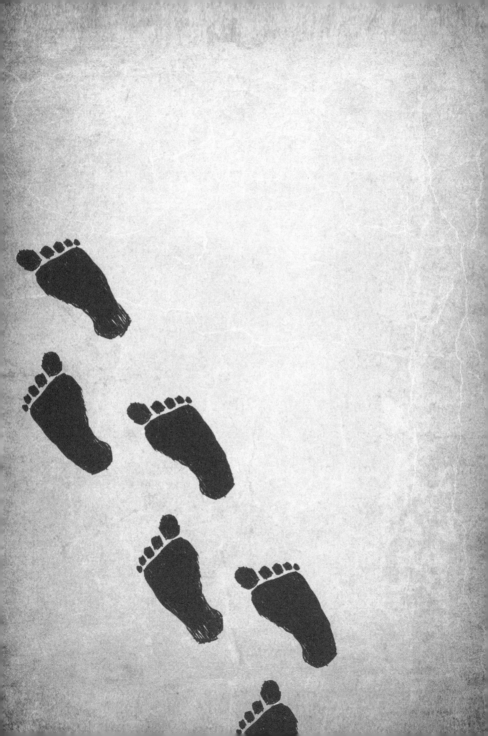

1

Ben Silverstein's bottom had gone numb.

He'd been sitting in a cold metal chair for two hours, playing checkers. In Ben's opinion, checkers was one of the most boring games ever invented, right up there with Go Fish and dominos. No laser cannons, no high-speed chases, no flashing lights or sirens. Just a wooden board, a pile of red buttons and a pile of black buttons. It was like playing a game from the caveman days.

And to make matters worse, Ben's opponent was Mrs. Froot, the oldest person in Buttonville. Her hair was so white it looked as if snow had fallen on her head. Her hearing aids were so squeaky it sounded as if two mice were living in her ears. And her eyeglass lenses were so thick that if a sunbeam shot through them, the whole senior center would catch fire. Ben secretly wished that would happen because it would give him an excuse to stop playing.

It was Tuesday, which was board game day at the Buttonville Senior Center. Ben didn't have anything else to do, so he'd agreed to spend the morning with his grandfather and the rest of the seniors. The air was stuffy with perfumes and medicated ointments.

"You're a good boy," his grandfather Abe Silverstein said from the next table, where he was playing Battleship with Mr. Filbert. "Isn't my grandson a good boy to play eleven games of checkers with Mrs. Froot?"

"King me!" Mrs. Froot commanded, strands of hair slipping from her bun.

"Yeah, okay," Ben grumbled, placing a red button on top of another red button. As it turned out, Mrs.

Froot was a bit of a ninja when it came to checkers. She had three kings on the board while Ben had zero.

Grandpa Abe leaned sideways and nudged Ben with his elbow. "How come you look so sad?"

"He's a sore loser," Mr. Filbert said. A military veteran, he'd come prepared for Battleship, dressed in his army jacket and medals. "No one likes to lose. If I don't take my pills, I lose my memory."

"I'm not sad about *losing*," Ben said, which was the truth. In the grand scheme of things, losing eleven games of checkers wasn't important. But some of the other things that had happened that summer were *definitely* important.

Like becoming an apprentice at Dr. Woo's Worm Hospital.

Thankfully, Dr. Woo didn't really take care of worms. Behind the walls of the old Buttonville Button Factory, Dr. Woo took care of Imaginary creatures. Only one week into his apprenticeship, Ben had already met a wyvern hatchling, a black dragon, a rain dragon, a leprechaun, a lake monster, a kelpie, two unicorns, and a sasquatch. And even though yesterday's apprenticeship hadn't introduced any new creatures, just an entire day spent plucking slugs from the sasquatch's fur, it had still been way better than sitting around playing old-fashioned board games.

But despite the great adventures in the Imaginary World, Ben couldn't forget the reason why his parents had sent him to stay with his grandfather in Buttonville. They needed time alone to discuss some "troubles." And that very morning, before heading to the senior center, Ben had received some bad news.

When Ben returned to Los Angeles at the end of the summer, his dad would be living in a different house. And that was the real reason why Ben felt sad.

"*Oy vey!*" Grandpa Abe exclaimed. "You sank my battleship!"

Four games later, Mrs. Froot dozed off in her chair. The checkers marathon was finally over.

"I'm pooped," Grandpa Abe said. "I need a nap, too." He put on his canvas hat and grabbed his cane. Then he waved good-bye to his friends. Once he and Ben were outside, he wrapped an arm around Ben's shoulder. "Listen to me, boychik. You have some big changes coming your way. What's important to remember is that your mother and your father will love you just as much in two houses as in one house. Sometimes things stay the same, sometimes they change. This is life!"

Ben knew his parents would still love him. But he didn't know how he'd feel having two bedrooms and two bus stops. It sounded very confusing.

Grandpa Abe's cane tapped as they walked down the front steps. "I know what you need to make you feel better. You need a big bowl of my matzo ball soup. It cures everything—common cold, influenza, even sadness. What's better than a fat matzo ball?"

"Okay," Ben said. He'd always liked matzo ball soup, but he didn't believe for a moment that it could cure his sad feelings.

"Ben!" a voice called.

"Hi, Pearl!" he called back.

A girl ran up the walkway, toward the senior center, her blond ponytail bouncing against her neck. "I ran all the way here," she explained, her cheeks bright red. "We've got a huge problem!"

2

WORM TROUBLE

Pearl Petal tended to get excited about things. Ben had only known her for a short time, but he'd already figured out that she wasn't the kind of girl who liked to sit quietly and watch life pass by. Her curiosity got her into trouble now and then, but that didn't stop her. She asked questions. She stepped boldly into the unknown. She was the most adventurous kid Ben had ever met.

Because Pearl also worked as an apprentice to

Dr. Woo, she and Ben shared a big batch of secrets. So when she hollered, "We've got a huge problem," his heart missed a beat.

"What's the matter?" Ben asked as Pearl skidded to a stop right in front of him. She stood so close that the toes of her sneakers touched his.

"You look like you've seen a ghost," Grandpa Abe said.

Ben wasn't worried about ghosts. Ghosts weren't real. But it was entirely possible that Pearl had seen something else, like a three-headed dog, a yeti, or a cyclops. Those things *were* real. Had something dangerous escaped the hospital, like the nasty child-eating kelpie they'd met in the basement pool?

"It...it...it wasn't a ghost." A big wad of gum appeared between Pearl's teeth as she chewed as fast as a squirrel. She glanced worriedly at Ben's grandfather. He didn't know any of their secrets. In fact, they'd been careful not to reveal their secrets to *anyone*. "Mrs. Mulberry was just at the store," Pearl explained. Pearl's family owned the Buttonville

Dollar Store. "She bought a little box so she could carry her worm."

"Martha Mulberry has a worm?" Grandpa Abe asked with surprise.

"She has a whole bunch of them," Pearl said, fidgeting as if there were ants in her shoes. "But one of them is sick."

Ben furrowed his brow. This was very worrisome news. Mrs. Mulberry, president of the Buttonville Welcome Wagon Committee, was the snoopiest person in town. She'd ordered red compost worms from a fancy gardening catalog, not because she owned a compost bin, but because she wanted an excuse to meet Dr. Woo. The only way to get inside Dr. Woo's hospital was to become an apprentice or to possess a sick worm that needed care.

"She's going to Dr. Woo's right now!" Pearl cried, squeezing Ben's arm so hard he thought it might snap in two.

"Ow," Ben said.

"Sorry." Pearl released her grip. "I'm just so worried. We have to stop her."

"Why would you keep Mrs. Mulberry from seeing Dr. Woo?" Grandpa Abe asked with a wag of his finger. "A sick worm should go to a worm doctor."

Ben's grandfather didn't understand what was at stake. If Martha Mulberry got inside the hospital, she'd ruin everything. She'd tell the whole world that Dr. Woo had a Portal into the Imaginary World. Dr. Woo would have to move to another town and leave Ben and Pearl behind!

Pearl stared at Ben, her green eyes super wide. He knew that look. She wanted him to make up a story. Ben wasn't a soccer star or a computer genius, but he did excel at one thing—creative storytelling. Some might call it *lying*.

Ben gathered his thoughts. He imagined Mrs. Mulberry storming the hospital, the way an invader might storm a castle. She'd pillage the whole place, looking in every corner, not for gold or jewels, but for information. Gossip was her career. He looked up at his grandfather and delivered an explanation. "We want to stop Mrs. Mulberry because we...we don't want to miss the worm examination. We're Dr. Woo's apprentices, so we need to learn as much as possible. That's our job."

"Yep," Pearl said with an eager nod. "It's our job."

Grandpa Abe shrugged. "My grandson, the future worm doctor. This I never expected." He pointed his cane down the sidewalk. "Well, what are you waiting for? Hurry!"

Like horses released from the starting gate, Ben and Pearl raced away. Pearl took the lead, as usual, her shiny basketball shorts flapping against her knees.

"I'll keep the soup warm for you," Grandpa Abe called.

"Thanks!" Ben called back.

Ben followed Pearl down Cedar Street and onto Cherry. They ran along the park, then took a right onto Maple, passing the duck pond and the closed gas station. Tall trees lined the road as it cut through the forest. Ben's side started to ache, but he wasn't about to complain. This was a million times better than playing checkers. He and Pearl were on a mission to protect Dr. Woo's secrets! One more bend in the road and they'd be able to see the hospital.

"Whoa!" Pearl cried as a yellow tennis ball rolled across her path, nearly tripping her.

If Ben had been back home in Los Angeles, he would have assumed that the ball had escaped from a tennis court or a golden retriever's mouth. But this was Buttonville, which was *nothing* like home. Ben stumbled, then grabbed the ball. It was drenched in something slimy.

"Slobber," he realized. Then he looked around and gasped. A huge head stuck out of the forest.

And it belonged to a dragon.

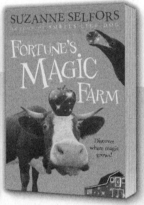
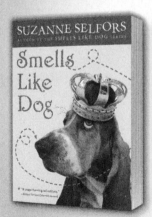

 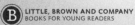

Welcome to
Ever After High!

Don't miss the first book in a new series! In *Next Top Villain*, Lizzie Hearts and Duchess Swan compete for top honors in General Villainy class—who will win?

Also check out *General Villainy: A Destiny Do-Over Diary*—the companion hextbook filled with activities straight out of the *Next Top Villain* story! Take General Villainy class with your favorite characters and rewrite the story: Accept thronework assignments from Mr. Badwolf, help Lizzie and Duchess choose different destinies, and more!

Find out more about Ever After High books at **everafterhigh.com**